ALSO BY

Other Northshore Noir Authors

Montana Carr

Secrets of Falls City
The Dark Corners of Falls City
Deception in Falls City

Liz McGillicuddy

Murder at Sunny Lake

To J

It's not that we don't love you, it's that you have no place
in this book.

WHEN THE TRUTH IS DONE

Aleelah Dixon

&

Emily Madison

Northshore Noir Press

This is a work of fiction. All names, characters and incidents are the product of the authors' imaginations. Any resemblance to real persons, living or dead, is entirely coincidental.

Northshore Noir Press
Toronto, Canada

www.northshorenoir.com

Contents

Chapter 1 — 2

Chapter 2 — 11

Chapter 3 — 20

Chapter 4 — 29

Chapter 5 — 37

Chapter 6 — 45

Chapter 7 — 52

Chapter 8 — 60

Chapter 9 — 67

Chapter 10 — 75

Chapter 11 — 83

Chapter 12 — 90

Chapter 13   97

Chapter 14   104

Chapter 15   111

Chapter 16   118

Chapter 17   126

Chapter 18   134

Chapter 19   141

Chapter 20   149

Chapter 21   156

Chapter 22   163

Chapter 23   171

Chapter 24   179

Chapter 25   187

Chapter 26   194

Chapter 27   202

Chapter 28   210

Chapter 29   217

Chapter 30   224

RUBY

CHAPTER 1

The room is white and sterile, the harsh fluorescent lights casting a clinical glow on the walls and ceiling. The bed is small and uncomfortable, sheets taut and scratchy against my skin. The machines beep and whirr, their screens displaying flashing numbers and lines.

I think I am somewhere between awake and dead. Usually there is "asleep" somewhere in there. But when you're in a hospital, and I think I am, there is only awake and dead. I think I...

Sorry about that. I think I wasn't alive, whatever that is. I have an idea it is morning. The voices around me sound chipper and full of energy. That's a morning thing. If the voices were higher and exhausted, I would think it was evening or night.

The faint yet distinct smell of disinfectant and sickness lingers in the air. The sheets and pillows carry a faint hint of bleach, and the overpowering scent of liniment fills my nostrils.

I'm not sure how long I've been here. Only a few hours, I hope. It had been dark. Now it was light. So maybe more than a few hours. I can't...

I keep falling asleep. Or dying. Not dying. I think the doctors would be much more concerned if I repeatedly died. I must be sleeping.

My mouth is dry and chalky, the taste of medicine and sickness lingering on my tongue.

For a minute or two, I can make out words, so I am now sure I am in a hospital. The words, spoken by different voices, were "organ, spinal, glass, dislocation, ligament, contusion." There were more words, but I stop listening.

I am not sure exactly what happened, but it sounds bad.

I am taken for tests and scans, which the doctors perform on me diligently. The machines beep and thrum as they analyze my body. They take pictures of my insides and measure the myriad of wounds I apparently sustained. As they work, they talk in hushed tones with each other, comparing notes and taking guesses at what needs to be done in order to help me. I keep my eyes closed. It's better that way.

The doctors come up with a plan of action that involves inserting screws into my bones to keep them together and wiring up my organs to get some kind of stability within my body. They also stitch up any open wounds or abrasions I may have suffered from the fall I took before coming here. The whole process takes hours, but eventually it is all done and I am wheeled back into the room where I had woken up earlier that morning - or perhaps it was yesterday - when everything was still dark outside.

Maybe I made that up, because it's still light out. I don't remember falling. What kinds of drugs are these people giving me?

"Ruby? Ruby Fisher? Can you hear me?"

They are blurry shapes above me, white coats with blurry faces. Fluorescent lights illuminate the room, making everything seem harsh and cold.

I could hear them, but it seemed like I couldn't answer. I must have grunted.

The metallic taste of blood coats my tongue, a reminder of the wounds I couldn't see. It makes my stomach churn, but I can't do anything about it.

"She needs some smelling salts."

"We don't use those anymore, Officer."

Officer? Was that a title or a last name? Either way, it wasn't a medical person, or they would have known. I grunted again. I think it was me, grunting. No one else would have a reason to grunt. Would they?

The air was antiseptic, stinging my nose as I struggled to take small breaths. Underneath, there was a faint scent of blood. Whose blood? Is that mine? I don't know what my blood smells like.

"Ruby. You are at Little Bluff Hospital."

That made sense. I lived outside Little Bluff. There was suddenly a blinding light in my eye, and I grunted again.

The voices around me are muffled and distant, like they are speaking through water. But there is a sense of urgency and concern in their tones.

"Ruby? Ruby? Can you hear me?" It was a woman's voice, and I could hear her. But I couldn't answer, didn't answer. Could I move?

"Dr. Galliano? She's moving a finger."

"Ruby, can you open your eyes for me?" Now, his voice was deep and resonant. I bet he's Dr. Galliano.

I thought about opening my eyes, but it all seemed too bright. Too much.

"Ruby, open your eyes."

Nope. I'm going back to wherever I was. Bye...

Hello. That didn't last long. Or did it? It was a different woman's voice now, asking me to open my eyes. I refused. I listened instead to the symphony of sounds in the hospital room.

Beeps and whirrs, hums and clicks of the machines that are plugged into me. They are like my orchestra, each instrument playing its own part in the song of medical care. A continuous bass line from an ECG monitor, a fluttering melody from the pulse oximeter, punctuated by the occasional beep of the ventilator.

I heard someone in the corner fiddling with a syringe. I could still feel my body, but it was strangely disconnected from my mind. I wanted to stay here forever in this lullaby of sounds–listening to nothing but the music of medical machines.

Huh. I can feel my body. That's good, isn't it? My body feels heavy and numb, as if it doesn't belong to me. I can feel cool, stiff sheets against my skin and the pressure of blankets draped over me.

"Ruby, wake up." It was a familiar voice. The Officer? It was very demanding, so I have decided this is a cop. A copper. A law man. I think that with a southern drawl. A constable. Oh, that was with an English accent. Let me try... Fuzz. Ha! I am sure I heard a groovy bass line.

"Ruby!"

"Officer, stop yelling at her!"

"That's a smirk. She can hear me."

"Everyone on the entire floor could hear you. Shush."

That was such a good shush. I wonder if she was a teacher once.

Am I being a petulant child now? Refusing to open my eyes or respond to the demands of a man child? Probably. Don't care. I like it here like this.

But I've only now remembered. I don't know why I am here. Someone said it was a hospital. That's right, Little Bluff Hospital, near where I live. Why am I here? And quite frankly, why can't I move?

The voices were like distant chimes, calling out to me from a foggy dreamscape. I feel myself being pulled back into consciousness, but it is a slow and arduous trip. Am I tripping? My mind feels like a tangled mess of wires, trying to make sense of the fragmented memories and sensations. I can't speak, but I could hear them, their voices cutting through the haze like sharp knives. Did I tell you that already?

As a child, I once hid in the trees for three hours, not moving. I was outside, playing with the kids from my street. We were in the woods behind our houses and I had decided to hide in the trees. The branches were so large that I could climb up one of them and be completely hidden by the leaves. So, I didn't move. Not so much as a leaf.

I won Hide 'n' Seek, but my parents were so angry. They'd called and called. I refused to budge. Three glorious hours.

I remember it smelled so amazing up there. Have you ever sat in a tree? You can smell the tree, the bark. Here, it stinks of cleaner and adulthood.

That's when something else comes back into focus - an ambulance ride. I was in an ambulance. Recently, I mean. Not because of Hide 'n' Seek. A sudden shock runs through my body as if something is coming alive inside me again.

Are they shocking me?

No, I don't think so. I am not going to open my eyes. They can't force me. Well, I guess they could pry my eyes open. Like that old movie where some guy forces some woman's eyes open so she can something something. You know the one.

"Doctor, how long until she regains consciousness?"

That must be the Officer again.

"Officer Pritchard, I've told you before. We don't know. The brain is a complex machine."

Yep, I was right. It was the cop. Officer Pritchard. Now what is a cop doing here? And why does he want me to wake up? I mean, I am awake. Maybe I'm going to lie here until he goes away.

Do cops go away? You'd think I'd know that. Not that I ever dated a cop, but I dated Diane, and she was always going to crime scenes. So, there's that. But let's not talk about her.

Someone pulled my sheet down. Now what? I hope it's not rude...

Nope. Not rude. They are tapping my knees, and I feel my legs spasm in response. Now someone has my arm in theirs. Ouch! Ow! They're hitting my elbows!

"Her reflexes are good."

"Her vitals are stable."

"But you still don't know why she won't wake up?"

That Officer Pritchard is very persistent. I don't understand why. What happened that makes it so important I wake up?

Panic spreads through my body. I can't stop it. Like that knee twitch, it's happening without my input. I don't know how I got here. My name is Ruby Fisher, I am 35, and I live alone in a little house outside Little Bluff, in Maine. So how'd I get here?

It's like I ought to know, but I shouldn't know. I can't know. It's like a door that I don't want to open because bad things are behind it. Terrible, unspeakable things.

I am Ruby. I am 35, and apparently I am prone to drama.

"Ruby! Wake the fuck up!"

Chapter 2

That Officer Pritchard is a rude man. But it worked. He startled my eyes open. I couldn't be awake dead anymore. Now I have to be awake alive.

"Ruby? I'm Officer Pri-"

"Officer Pritchard! Step back!" That was Dr. Galliano's voice.

I'd like to reach out and take his hand. Thank him for getting Rude Boy away from me. But my hand doesn't move.

"Ruby. I'm Dr. Galliano. You were in a car accident. You're in Little Bluff Hospital."

The car accident part is new. I don't think there was a car accident.

"Ruby? Can you raise your hand for me?"

I can now that I am awake alive. I raise my arm and get complimented. I like that. I don't get a lot of compliments.

"How about the other arm? Can you wiggle your toes?"

There was a breeze up my legs as the nurse, probably a nurse, pulled back the sheets. It took me a moment to realize she wouldn't cover me back up until I wiggled. I wiggled. I was covered.

"We're going to sit you up. Are you ready?"

I wasn't, but I wasn't in control either, so they raised the backrest of the bed, and I sat up.

"How do you feel?"

The nurse seemed nice. Dr. Galliano too. Not Officer Rude Boy.

"Okay?" That came out of me more as a question than an answer. But since I'd been in a car accident, I couldn't be sure.

"Do you remember what happened?"

"Doc, please keep your questions related to medical stuff. Okay?"

Officer Rude Boy's "okay?" was much more assured and confident than mine.

"Officer Pritchard, please let me conduct my assessment. With my patient. Mine."

Were these two men fighting over me? Ew. Except Officer Pritchard fell silent and sullen, and Dr. Galliano asked me more questions. I won't bore you with my medical status, because the only people who care about medical statuses are old people and ill people. And mostly they care about their own, not mine.

Hm. I think Officer Rude Boy is rubbing off on me. Sorry about that.

Let me say, I was well enough to be questioned by the cop.

"Ma'am, I'm Officer Pritchard. Badge 471. Little Bluff Police. Traffic Services. Do you recall why you're here?"

"The doctor said it was a car accident."

"Yes ma'am. But what do you remember about it, yourself?"

I took a deep breath in and tried hard to remember what happened.

"My name is Ruby Fisher. I am 35 years old. I live outside Little Bluff. Uh. I work at Peachtree Fabrication in the-"

"I meant about the accident. What do you remember about the car accident?"

Well, you should have said that to begin with.

"Okay, sorry. Let me think... When did I crash? Knowing that might make it a little clearer."

"You crashed your car last night."

"And it's morning now? Okay, okay, that's helpful. I-"

"One moment." Officer Rude Boy said as he held up a finger on one hand and reached for his phone with another. I can't believe he took a phone call while I was speaking. Rude. Boy.

"I'm sorry ma'am. Change of plans. I've been told that someone else is taking over the case. Have a good day."

And then he was gone. Poof. I looked at the nurse, and she shrugged and shook her head. She fiddled with the IV that was attached to my arm, making sure it was dripping. It was.

She asked me pain questions, comfort questions and existing medication questions.

"Six. I could use a blanket, please. None."

The woman before me exuded a warm, motherly aura. She had thoughtfully placed the blanket in the warmer, and now, as she pulled it over me, its heat enveloped my body like a gentle embrace. My eyelids grew heavy and I could feel myself drifting off into a peaceful slumber. The comforting warmth of the blanket made me feel safe and content, like I was being cradled in love. Sleep overtook me as I melted into the cozy cocoon of the soft fabric.

"Ruby Fisher?"

I snorted awake. I was still in the hospital, still sitting at a 45 degree angle. My blanket is human warm, not blanket oven warm.

"Yes, I'm Ruby Fisher." Like it says on my wrist.

Hm. I am still channeling Officer Rude Boy.

"My name is Detective Scott O'Reilly. This is my partner, Detective Francine Temple. Little Bluff Police Department."

"About the car accident?" We shook hands as best I could. Detective Francine's hand was lovely. Detective Scott's hand was...not.

"Yes ma'am."

"Please call me Ruby."

"Great. You can call me Scott."

"Francine." I like her eyes. His eyes are snake eyes. Hers are mouse eyes.

"We had a brief conversation with Officer Pritchard. But we'd like to hear from you."

"I really don't remember much. About the car accident, I mean. It's not like I have amnesia. I know who I am."

"Tell us about the accident, Ruby."

Detectives Scott and Francine sat down in the two chairs next to my bed. I noticed that Detective Francine had a notebook in her hand, while Detective Scott had a file folder. They looked like they meant business.

"So, Ruby, can you tell us about what happened last night?" Do they have to keep asking that question?

I took a deep breath and tried to remember. It all seemed so hazy.

"Well, I was driving home from work. I work at Peachtree Fabrication. It's out by Little Bluff."

"Yes, we know," said Francine as she scribbled something in her notebook.

"I must have fallen asleep at the wheel or something because the next thing I remember is waking up here in the hospital."

"Do you have any recollection of what caused you to fall asleep?"

I racked my brain but couldn't come up with anything concrete. "No, not really. It's all kind of a blur."

"What about before the accident? Were you feeling tired or ill?" Detective Francine leaned in closer. She is very attractive.

I thought back to yesterday and shook my head. "No, I felt fine. Tired from work. No! I remember driving. It was night, but it was cool. It's that time of year. I would have had the windows rolled up. I..." And that's where things fell apart. I have flashes, but I'm not sure of what's true and what's wrong. I was suddenly very aware that saying the wrong thing could get me into trouble. I watch enough police shows to know there are no Detectives in Traffic

Services. Once you start talking, they're in. They listen to every word, then pick and choose what suits them.

Diane once told me–wait, why am I bringing her up again?–Diane told me to never ever speak to the police without an attorney. Even if you're a witness. Because maybe you think you're a witness, but they think you're a suspect. And those Detectives will question you. They've been doing this for years. But you? Innocent you? You've probably never been interviewed by police. I never have, at any rate. Until now.

"Where was I?"

"You were driving in the evening–"

"She said it was night."

Now I really liked Detective Francine.

"You were driving at night. The windows were rolled up."

"Right, yes. I think so. It was cold. Probably. I don't exactly remember the last few days so clearly. But yes, the windows would have been rolled up."

"Where were you going?"

"Where did I crash?"

"Old Weller Road."

"Ah! I was either coming or going. I live on Yurton Road. Off Old Weller."

"128 Yurton?"

"Oh yes. You know that?"

"It's on your car registration. So were you coming or going?"

I shrugged and sighed more under my blanket. I wondered if I should have an attorney. I know my address is on my registration, but I don't like Detective Scott's attitude. I have to wonder what this is all about.

"What direction was the car facing?"

"East."

"Was I east or west of Yurton?"

"East."

"I was coming home. You know, this is a little confusing. Can you tell me what happened?"

Detective Scott and Detective Francine exchanged looks, and Detective Scott nodded. Detective Francine was allowed to tell me. I don't like how he controls her.

"You were driving eastbound on Old Weller when your car went off the road. You went into a ditch and tipped the car."

So what? That's what I wanted to say or loud. Who cares? Why is this so important that Detectives are required? I was getting angry, and a ringing started in my ears. I tried hard to breathe normally, but it suddenly seemed–.

The nurse came rushing in, scooting the Detectives to the corner of the room. The ringing was some kind of alarm, a monitor. "I am so sorry," she mumbled as she swapped a full IV bag for the empty one that fed into my arm. It took a few minutes of fussing, pressing buttons, and checking the line.

"Detectives, is this really necessary?" That nurse is my hero.

"Yes ma'am. We'll try to be quick."

It seemed good enough for her, and I was back to talking with Detectives Scott and Francine.

"You were saying?"

"No, no. You were telling me I tipped the car in a ditch. Is there more to the accident?"

I didn't like the look they exchanged.

CHAPTER 3

So here I am, hurt in a car accident, police Detectives talking to me. I think things can't get worse, and then there was that look between them. As if they think I am lying. I think things can't get worse, and Diane bursts in. Her face is flushed with panic, her hand clutching the door frame for support.

"Ba-Ruby? Ruby, what happened?"

She came rushing over to my bedside. I opened and closed my mouth a few times, but didn't make a sound. A chill ran through my body as I feel myself being scrutinized by the Detectives. Diane grips my shoulder in a comforting gesture that is as hollow as she is.

"How did you get here?"

"I drove. Who are you two?"

"Detectives O'Reilly and Temple. Who are you?"

"Diane Emerat. Ruby's friend. The hospital called. Ruby, what happened? They said you were in an accident."

Without fail, she always answered her own questions before I even had the chance to open my mouth. I hated that about her mother, too. Eunice used to do that. Maybe apples don't fall far from trees. No. I take that back. It is one of the many things I loved about her. Though this particular habit never failed to drive me up the wall with frustration. No matter how much I adored her, there were moments when her actions left me feeling a tinge of annoyance. I'm not at my best when I am annoyed.

She let go of me and gripped the bar that is designed to stop me from tumbling out. Even though we'd never been in this exact position before, we both knew the dance.

"The Detectives were telling me there was an accident, but I don't remember too well."

"Is she under arrest?"

Diane had a tenacious nature when it came to my time, demanding every bit of it without compromise. She would not settle for anything less than complete devotion and attention.

"No. Should she be?"

"No, I... Sorry. Sorry about that."

I don't remember Diane ever saying "sorry" to me. Certainly never twice in a row.

"Let me start again. I'm Diane Emerat. I'm a medicolegal death investigator in Peterson County. I've heard of you both, Detectives. Homicide, aren't you?"

You'd have been able to knock me down with a feather if I wasn't already down. Homicide Detectives.

"We are."

My heart sank. "Was someone else hurt?" I know I said those words, but they sounded like they came from a little girl.

"Stop. Would you mind if we chat? The two of us?"

"Who are you to her?"

"We're best friends. I've known Ruby for years."

"Is that why the hospital called?"

"Yes. I'm still your emergency contact. You really scared me."

"I'm really scared."

Diane stretched out her arms and turned her Christ pose toward the door. "I'd like a few minutes. To check in. Between besties."

Neither Detective moved.

"Please." Oh, there it was. That tone. Unmistakable. Even the Detectives didn't mistake that tone. That was the DO IT OR ELSE tone. The Detectives stood up and headed to the door.

"We'll get coffee. Either of you want anything from the hospital cafeteria?" Detective Francine was thoughtful.

"No, neither of us. Thank you."

The Detectives stepped out and Diane settled into the chair beside me. Before speaking, she scoped out the room. It was only the two of us, and it was a small room. But being this deeply in the gay closet meant you lived a life that made you look for other eyes and ears before speaking.

She leaned over the sturdy anti-tumble bar, her hand gently caressing my face as if trying to soothe away any pain or worry. Her voice was filled with concern.

"Oh baby, what happened?" The soft touch of her fingertips against my skin sent a warm sensation through me, easing any tension I may have been holding onto. In that moment, I felt safe and loved, knowing she was there for me.

"The Detectives said I was in an accident. But they never told me they were Homicide. Did I...?"

"Not that I heard. I heard about your accident, though I didn't know it was you. Not until I got the call from the hospital. What do you remember?"

"Not much at all. I woke up in the hospital."

"Were you drinking?"

Of course I'd been drinking.

"What day is today?"

"Thursday."

She broke my heart thirteen days ago. Thirteen days ago, she sat next to me on my couch and said she's fallen in love with Velma. What kind of cartoonish name is that? Velma was her secretary, ten years younger by my estimate. Velma who had no problem letting the entire world know she was a lesbian. Velma, who had probably never spent a single day in the closet.

For weeks, a cold tension had been building between us before the harsh reality was finally revealed - she no longer wanted me. Her once warm and affectionate demeanor had gradually turned distant and uninterested. And when I was starting to accept it, she suddenly showed interest in me again after almost two weeks of silence. The rollercoaster of emotions left me dizzy and unsure of where we stood now. It was as if the winds had shifted direction without warning, leaving me struggling to keep my footing.

"Yes, I've been drinking. Every night since you left me."

"Ruby, what were you thinking?"

"I don't know. Nothing at all, I suppose."

"That was always your problem. You never thought anything through."

"If by that you mean, I never thought about what it would take to cheat on you with my secretary, you're right."

"Don't start. Our relationship was over."

"Over her."

"Over before Velma and I."

"She's not for you. I am."

"You were. Once. Have you...have you told them about us?"

Was that why she came? After she heard about my accident, she'd thought only about being found out? I didn't have to answer. The Detectives walked in and I fell silent. She knew I'd said nothing, or I'd have kept talking.

"Ladies, I hope we aren't interrupting?"

"No, not at all. It's almost four o'clock. I'll be leaving soon. Please, don't let me stop you from doing whatever you're doing. As I said previously, I'm a medicolegal death investigator. I know the importance of speaking with people after an event."

It was then Detective Scott decided to put me out of my misery. My car had gone off-road, into a ditch and hit a pole. It sounded really terrible. They think it was sometime late Wednesday night. I wasn't found until early Thursday morning. A cleaner on his way to work spotted my car and called for an ambulance.

"I was there all night?" It seemed surreal. I wracked my brain.

"Do you remember it now?"

I looked around at the ceiling tiles as if they held the secret. It was something I've done since I was a kid. There was a flash, an image. Then it was gone.

"What is the last thing you remember?"

Both Detectives gave Diane a look. She should leave the questions to them. But it didn't surprise me at all. She always needed to be in control.

"I remember being at work–"

"Where is that?"

"Peachtree Fabrications. We make kitchenware. Cupboard handles, tableware, kitchen rails. That kind of thing. I work in the sales office. Entering data, typing out orders, that kind of thing."

"And you remember working on Wednesday? At Peachtree Fabrications?"

"Yes. Let's see, after work, I... hmm."

"Did you go out for a drink with your co-workers?"

Diane laughed. She could be cruel that way. She knows I don't socialize with people at work. I don't socialize with anyone.

"No. I'd have gone straight home. I...I'm quite certain I made myself a pasta salad. Yes. I distinctly remember grating the Parmesan. Parmigiano-Reggiano, the real stuff."

"Okay, so you were at work, and you went home and had dinner. Were you alone?"

I looked out the window for answers this time. They still weren't there. I could see Diane's reflection in the window. She had such beautiful long blonde hair. Not like my scrambled up mop.

"I certainly think so."

"Look, it's clear she can't remember, why don't you drop it?"

"Ms. Emerat, please let us work. We don't want to upset Ruby."

I smiled. Detective Francine to my rescue again. I like her. She has short black hair, the opposite of Diane. Detective Scott also has short black hair, but I don't care much about him.

"Ruby? Did you have a dinner guest?"

"No. I am certain I ate alone."

"You ate alone, and you didn't go out that evening with co-workers for a drink? Not before or after dinner?"

"Do you ever hang out with co-workers? Maybe not that night, but any time?"

I looked into Detective Scott's hard eyes. I didn't much like that question.

CHAPTER 4

"I don't like these questions. They are too open ended."

I wanted to scream at Diane to shut up, but I didn't dare.

"Ma'am, you're here because we allow it. Please don't interrupt."

"It might help me remember more if you can be a little more exact."

Detective Francine threw her empty coffee cup in the garbage. Detective Scott had tucked his under his chair. I bet he won't throw it out. That's the kind of man he is.

"Do you know Clive Benning?"

A bolt of panic surged through me as I stared at the flashing numbers on the heart rate monitor. My heartbeat was accelerating, threatening to climb off the charts. Frantically, I reached for one of the foam electrodes and ripped it off, the red line on the monitor disappearing in an instant. I took a deep breath, willing my racing pulse to slow down before anyone noticed my momentary distress. The room suddenly felt stifling and claustrophobic, my skin slick with sweat under the harsh lights. I tried to calm myself.

"No. Did he run me off the road?"

"No. He works at Peachtree too. A co-worker."

I shook my head. I felt like my whole body was shaking. Sweat dripped down my forehead and my hands trembled from the adrenaline rush. It wasn't easy, but I had managed to regain control over my body before anyone noticed my momentary lapse of composure. I looked at my fingers. They were trembling, so I stuck my hands under the blanket. There are 250 or so people who work at Peachtree, and of all those people, I knew maybe ten. Clive was one. "I don't know Clive Benning. Clive was not at my home for dinner. Ever."

Damn. Was that the question they had asked me about Clive? Diane was trying her best not to interrupt. I could see she was almost shaking with desire to intrude. There was a time when I wanted to see Diane shake, but not right–

"Did he run her off the road?"

I'd asked that question a second ago. Was she not paying attention? A withering look from Detective Scott was the only answer she got.

"You work at Peachtree, and so did Clive. But you don't know him?"

"No. What's he got to do with my accident?"

"We don't think he had anything to do with your accident."

"Hey! What are you playing at?"

"Ma'am, we're going to have to ask you to leave."

"No. I...I'll go get a coffee. I'll stop interrupting." As Diane stood from her chair, its rusted metal legs screeched against the linoleum floor. Turning towards me with a gentle smile on her face, she exuded warmth and kindness. Anxious butterflies fluttered in my stomach as Diane exited the room, leaving me alone with two sharp-eyed Homicide Detectives.

Under the scrutiny of the Detectives' piercing gazes, my confidence began to falter. The fluorescent lights overhead cast a stark white glow over us, adding to the tense atmosphere of the room. Every sound seemed amplified, from the scratch of pencils on notepads to the distant hum of traffic outside. I couldn't help but feel like a suspect under interrogation, even though I was innocent.

"Okay. Let's try again. You don't work with Clive?"

"No. I really work with the sales team. They give me their orders, and I enter the orders into the system."

"And where do you do that?"

"My office, if you can call it that, is really only a corner of the open-plan sales room. There are no walls to separate us, only desks and computers scattered about in, I guess you could call it organized chaos. It's a small team - me, Cath, Bill, Sam and Doug - and we all worked together to input the orders that came in from our clients. They are the only people I see every day. You don't have to take my word for it though, go ahead and ask any of them - Cath, Doug, Bill or Sam. They'll all tell you the same thing."

"Not with Clive?"

"No. Where did Clive work?"

"The floor. He's a machinist with Peachtree."

Detective Francine explained that Clive worked for Peachtree for three years, but was recently suspended for harassing other employees. He sexually harassed the women and physically harassed the men. An all around rotten guy.

"From what we understand, from talking with other people at Peachtree, he was a piece of work. Suspended first thing Monday morning. We spoke with Human Resources."

"Grace." There was only one person who worked in Human Resources. She was an old, sour busybody who tried to pry the most private information from me. I caught her once listening to a conversation I had with Diane. It didn't matter, we are—were very cautious. Always. But the old hag sure did try.

"Yes. Grace Horowitz. She told us he was suspended. He was caught peeping into the women's washroom."

It did not at all surprise me that Grace would hand over gossip at the drop of a hat. "How'd he do that? Is that even possible?"

"Yes, it's possible and he was caught. And suspended. There was a peephole in the last stall. Drilled through the wall from the men's room on the other side."

To my surprise, Detective Francine kept talking when the nurse came in and took my vitals. This was a nurse I hadn't seen before. I tuned out Detective Francine's voice for a few moments while the nurse murmured questions in my ear. How was my pain? Could I please move fingers and toes? How is my vision?

I guess I passed all the tests because she left me alone with the Detectives. I tuned back in to hear more stories about Clive.

"I'm sorry. I don't understand what Clive has to do with me?"

"We aren't sure he does. Nothing concrete."

Diane walked back in as Detective Scott spoke. "Nothing concrete? About what?" That woman couldn't help herself.

"They have nothing concrete tying me to Clive." Those words were both a relief and a dagger.

"You didn't know him?"

"No."

"He's dead."

I gasped. I couldn't help myself. I felt my lips open. Felt the cool air draw past my lips. The noise sounded like a gunshot to me. I don't know how loud it really was, but loud enough to make everyone look at me.

I began to tremble, then shake. My blood pressure went up. Or down. I'm not sure which, but it set off an alarm that brought the nurse. She gave everyone except me a very dirty look. To me, she was compassion and kindness. She asked me to please hold up the blanket, like so. It gave me a modest curtain as she reattached the foam electrode and fixed the cuff and set me right. Then she left me alone with sharks.

With all eyes on me, I spoke. "Did I...did I hit him with my car? Oh God did I kill a man?"

Diane reached out and grabbed my shoulder, waving her other hand in the air. I think she was trying to swipe the words away. I did the only thing I could think of. I began to wail.

"No, no, no. You didn't hit him."

I tried to catch my breath but ended up choking on my own phlegm.

"Why would you scare us like that?"

Us? You and I are "us" now?

"We're trying–" Detective Scott cut himself off when his phone buzzed. He read the message before continuing. "Trying to find out what happened to him."

"I'm very confused. I'm confused and tired." I really was. This was exhausting.

"Clive Benning died in his own home."

"Nothing to do with the car accident?"

"We are still trying to get information. It's basic information."

"Oh! Oh! You think she might have seen something? That's it! Isn't it? Oh ba–Ruby, try to remember. Try hard to remember what happened that night."

"Oh for the love of God, woman! Please stop. One more time and you're out."

"I'm confused. Did I witness something to do with Clive?"

I don't think I've ever seen a more frustrated man than Detective Scott in that moment. I wasn't surprised when he quickly stood up and walked out. Diane can be aggravating like that. Detective Francine followed on her partner's heels. I wish I had a partner like that.

"What did you see?"

"Not you too. Nothing. I saw nothing."

CHAPTER 5

It took only a few minutes for the Detectives to return to my hospital room. I think it's funny that Diane can alienate people so quickly. I wonder what I saw in her. Why I am so desperate to keep her. Why I want her back.

"Let's start all over again. Diane, please, don't talk. You can be here for support, but that's all. Okay?"

"Okay."

"Ruby, let's go over Wednesday night again. You need to tell us. You worked, you went home, you had supper alone. You remember all that."

"Yes."

"Then you went out. We know that because you said your car was pointing in the direction of home when you were found. Now, there was a 911 call from someone who saw your car. That was at 5:46 a.m. We need to know what happened between the time you finished dinner, and the time you were found."

I took a sip of tepid water that had been sitting out all day. It had that horrible flavor to it. You know the flavor. But I took a second sip. My throat burned with every swallow, but I knew I needed time to figure out what happened next. So I closed my eyes and forced myself to take another drink, trying to ignore the lingering aftertaste. It must have worked.

"I had supper. And... and I thought I might like to talk to someone. I guess I was feeling a little lonely. I live alone, you see."

"You were lonely, and you got into your car to go somewhere."

"Yes. I remember putting the radio on. Talk radio. I like to hear the voices. Hear someone talking."

"I live alone too. I get it."

"Where did you drive to?"

"I..."

"Yes?"

"I went to a bar." I covered my mouth with my hand, trying to stop the words from coming out. But they were already out. I'd gone to a bar. I'd been drinking. They probably tested my blood alcohol level.

"Do you know which bar?"

"Did I crash because I was drunk?"

"No! No way! Not Ruby. You don't know her like I do. She'd never drive drunk. Not ever." A glare from Detective Scott shut her down. But she was right. Not only would I never drive drunk, nobody knew me like Diane. And no one knew her like me. That's how couples are sometimes.

"No. Your blood alcohol level was negligible. Like maybe you'd had one drink."

I swallowed hard. "I drove to The Grab Bar."

"The Grab Bar?"

"That's it. Get out. Diane, out now. Go." Detective Scott pointed to the door. Detective Francine stood up and took her by the arm and took her out into the hall. They'd had about enough of her, and I knew the feeling.

"What do you remember about The Grab Bar?"

"I..." There was no point in dragging this out. "I went to the bar to have a drink, have some conversation."

"Why that bar in particular?" It wasn't close to my home, it wasn't a first option for most decent women. The Grab Bar was a pick-up place, if they still call them that. Probably not. The word is hook-up. The word where men and women meet each other for sex. Now, that's men and women. I prefer women, and that's not where women loving women go. But I went there.

"I guess I wanted some company. I've heard about that bar."

"From who?"

"Someone at work. Cath, I think."

"What happened at the bar?"

"It's not exactly what I thought. I was hoping to talk, but the music was loud. Too loud. And it's not the kind of music you can dance to."

"Did you stay long?"

Detective Francine was back. "Did you have a drink?"

"Yes."

"What kind?"

"A wine spritzer."

"Did you buy it, or did someone buy it for you?"

"I'm not sure. It was one drink, does it matter?"

"It does. We need to establish that you were there. It's a police thing. I'm sure your medicolegal death investigator friend has told you that details are everything. It fills up a report for the higher ups. Now, did you order from the bartender?"

"I think... No. Someone bought my drink for me."

The Detectives looked at each other. I looked out the window. I am starting to not like this at all. I feel trapped. Like a rabbit staring down a couple of hungry coyotes.

Detective Scott's phone dinged. He walked out, leaving me with Detective Francine. Maybe she would be easier to talk to if she was alone. I like her eyes. They have wrinkles around them when she smiles. Not laugh lines, because she certainly was not laughing. And this isn't a laughing matter. But I like the lines around her eyes.

"Someone bought me my drink." I swallowed hard. Here it comes. Here comes the goddamned truth.

"Yes?"

"Yes. I was lonely and I went to The Grab Bar and I had a drink. One drink. I... I ran into someone from work. But you know that. Don't you?"

"We do."

Diane once told me that the police never ask a question they don't already have the answer to. I've heard that on TV, too.

"And you know it was Clive Benning."

"We do."

It felt terrible to say I'd had a drink with Clive. "It makes it sound like I'm lying. I'm not lying. It's so hazy. It's taking time to remember."

"I have time."

Detective Scott came back into the room. Detective Francine told him what I told her. I was glad I didn't have to repeat myself. It was getting boring, so I went on.

"I remember the music was really loud and it seemed confusing. So when I saw a familiar face, I went over to say 'hi.' I didn't know his name, but I knew his face. Clive has a reputation at work. All the ladies have to keep an eye out for him."

"All the ladies?"

"I don't think any of us are safe with him. Not alone, anyway. I... Cath told me that Brenda fell for him. But he broke her heart."

The Detectives both sat up when I said Brenda's name. "Do you know Brenda's last name?"

"Gallagher. Brenda Gallagher. She works the metal sheet fabrication line. Cath said she saw them together, out the back of the building. They were making out."

Detective Scott walked out. I knew what he was doing. He was telling someone on his team to go talk to Brenda Gallagher. I hope I didn't throw her under the bus.

"Back to the bar."

"I feel like this is getting overblown."

"When you have nothing to go on, every morsel is important."

I told them I didn't go home for dinner. I told them I met up with Clive after work. We went to a diner, then the bar. We meet up at the bar because we were both driving, but we were together before the bar.

"What's the diner?"

"Mildred's. At the gas station off Highway 23. The waitress was a girl with light hair. On the younger side. We both had hamburgers. Paid cash. Went to The Grab Bar. For a drink."

I figured they had video from the bar, so I had to come clean. "Yes. I'm sorry I wasn't upfront about Clive. It's...well, I don't want a reputation. Cath can be quite the gossip."

"What would she gossip about?"

"Clive and I were necking. I...I've never kissed a man with a beard. It's like kissing a teddy bear. Not that I know what that's like. It's what I imagine."

"Necking with Clive."

"But he was being weird."

"Weird how?"

"I close my eyes when I kiss someone. But every time I opened my eyes, his eyes were open. And he was not looking at me. He was looking past me."

"At what?"

"He said someone was watching us kiss. I didn't see who."

"Watching you?"

"Yes."

"But you never saw the person."

"No. But Clive was so freaked out, he left. And then I left. I saw him pull out of the parking lot. Then I drove home. Tried to drive home."

"Then you crashed."

CHAPTER 6

I'm tired, and the police have been asking me questions for a long time. The fluorescent lights buzzed above me, casting a sickly yellow glow that made my head ache. I hate hospital lighting.

My stomach rumbled loudly, reminding me that it was dinner time. Finally, after what seemed like hours of questioning, I was given a covered plate and a small milk container.

"Can I eat?"

"Yes please. Maybe we should grab a bite in the cafeteria."

"Sure, yeah. We'll be back in a little while. We'll let you eat in peace."

The aroma of warm food wafted from under the lid, tempting my growling stomach. The creamy white milk swirled gently in the plastic container, promising to soothe my parched throat. I sat back and looked my meal. It was lukewarm turkey slices, something like deli slices. Processed. I pulled off the foil off my plastic milk box and took a sip. Lukewarm. A mouthful of carrot matchsticks, a mouthful of mashed potatoes, a mouthful of turkey. Wash it all down with milk. Once again, I am eating alone.

I couldn't understand it. Despite my best efforts to be a kind and welcoming person, my shyness had always held me back, thanks to Diane's constant criticism. And when I was lost in my thoughts, she appeared before me with impeccable timing, like a villain entering the scene of a play at the perfect moment to cause chaos.

"Oh, baby. My sweet baby. What happened?"

I was surprised when she leaned over the bars to hug me. I won't lie: it felt good. But then it changed and her fingers became steel traps and she started hurting my arm.

"Tell me everything. Now."

I hate that look in her face. It's scary. I wondered if I should press the call button, and as my hand reached out, the Detectives opened the door and walked in.

Diane is spring-loaded. She released me, stood straight and coughed all in one swift motion. She'd developed the cough as a way to cover up movement. If she was caught doing something wrong, like kissing me, she'd cough so that whoever saw would be able to chalk it up to that.

"You should wear a mask if you have something contagious."

Detective Francine really did care about me.

"It's something in my throat."

"Same rules as before, Diane. No interruptions."

"Ruby, tell us about your drive home. About the crash."

I looked quickly at Diane, then Detective Francine, and spoke. "Let's see. I pulled out of the parking lot. I didn't see a car coming and we almost hit. But I stopped in time and then I almost got hit from behind by whoever was coming out of the parking lot behind me. It was horns in front and horns behind."

"Nerve wracking."

"What can you tell us about either car?"

"Not much. The one on the road was silver or white. The one behind was dark. Blue or black maybe. I couldn't tell you what kind."

"She's not good with cars."

"Yes. So I left The Grab Bar and headed home."

"What roads did you take?"

"Probably Decker Road to Highway 21, over to 23, then Old Weller Road."

"Probably? Do you remember exactly?"

"Not really. But that's the route I always take–"

Diane's eyes widened and nearly shot out of her head. It was comical, really.

"– from work. I pass The Grab Bar all the time. You know, one thing I remember..." I scratched my head, pulling the IV a little.

"What do you remember?"

"Oh geez. It's coming back. It's... I drove north on Decker, and this car was behind me. He had his high beams on and it was shining in my eyes."

"He?"

"You saw the driver?"

"No. I assume. 'They', I'll say 'they.' They had the beams on. A truck passed us going the other direction, and they flashed their lights at the person behind me. I turned east onto 21, and sped up. But the car also sped up and passed me. I think that's it for them. I went north on 23, and east again on Old Weller."

"And this is a common route?"

"Every day."

"Keep going."

"I turned onto Old Weller. But someone was behind me."

"Is that unusual?"

"Yes. There are only ten or a dozen houses on Old Weller. It's rare to run into a neighbor."

"And you live on Old Weller?"

"She lives at 128 Yurton."

I wonder how much more Detective Scott will take before he shoots Diane for interrupting.

"You crashed on Old Weller."

"Whereabouts in Old Weller?"

"Six hundred yards east of Yurton. There's a culvert, and a telephone pole. You went into the culvert and hit the pole."

"The pole with the cross on it?"

"How do you know about that pole, Diane?"

Her eyes flickered left and right, like she's been caught in a lie. But it wasn't a lie. There was a white cross on that pole. A young man had driven smack into it, died instantly. If I hit that same pole, I guess I was really lucky.

"Diane?"

"Well, Ruby and I are best friends. I've been to her house. I know the pole."

"What else do you remember, Ruby? Do you remember hitting the pole?"

I scratched my head and took another sip of terrible water. "Could someone get me some fresh water?" No one moved, so I put the cup down. What a bunch of meanies.

"I was on Old Weller... there were lights. Car head-lights."

"Behind you?"

"In front. God! I remember now! The car in front came way over and I had to yank. Yank the steering wheel." I held out my hands as if I had hold of a steering wheel, and turned hard to the right.

"Did you–"

"The sound!" I put my hands up to cover my ears. "There were horrible sounds. So loud. Metal. Someone drove into me! Oh God, why would they do that?"

"Someone ran you off the road?"

"Scraped my car and ran me off the road."

"Then you hit the pole."

"It was really loud. Bam! And then I saw stars , bright lights. Then. Nothing. No. There was something. Some-one knocked on the window. No! Broke the window. The glass fell on me. I... I heard...an angel? That sounds silly. I don't believe in angels."

"I bet it was an angel. Angels saved you."

Diane and her damned angels. She had one on her dash-board to watch her drive. She had one on her mantel at home to watch her watch TV. She used to have one in the bedroom, but I put my foot down. She'd put it away whenever I came over.

"Something wet."

"Wet?"

"I think I wet myself. But it was by my head, so I'm not sure." I touched my head. No bandages. "But then nothing. I could hear nothing. Everything was hazy. Then black." I started to tear up, and Detective Francine gave me some tissues. In response, Diane put her arm on my shoulder and rubbed.

"What next? After the black?"

"Light. The sun was coming up and I woke up. I thought it was the weirdest dream ever. A man was asking me my name. I don't know what I said."

"You started singing."

"I can't sing. That poor man. Who was he?"

"He found you, and called 911."

"Oh! I remember the sirens. Wee-ooh, we-ooh. I...the fire fighters. They covered me up and pulled me out and put me in the ambulance."

The Detectives asked again, and I told them again. I drove home, someone cut me off, I drove into the pole. An angel came to me laughing. I'd forgotten that the first time around, but the angel laughed. And the man and the ambulance. I think I got it right.

CHAPTER 7

My head is buzzing. I tell them my head is buzzing. The Detectives sit there, but Diane leaves and brings a nurse back. I tell her my head is buzzing. She says something, but I shake my head, wave my hands near my ears, and shrug. That's the international sign for 'I can't hear you.'

I watch as she shooed out the Detectives and Diane. I put my head back and breathe. "They're exhausting."

"It's not my place to tell you what to do. But if I was in the hospital and the Detectives talked to me for hours and hours, I'd have a lawyer. That's me."

"I hear ya. I don't want them to think I have something to hide."

"Oh, they think you're hiding something. Look, people lie to cops, doctors and lawyers. So cops, doctors and lawyers go around assuming people are lying to them. So those Detectives think you are hiding something. It's in their nature, it's part of what they do."

"I don't remember. Has the doctor told me what's wrong with me?"

"You were in a car accident."

Now that made me laugh. "I meant, what's broken? I think I remember some surgery? Screws to connect my bones?"

"No. Dr. Galliano did go over it with you. I'll get him for you." The moment she stepped out, the others came back in.

"The doctor is on his way."

"We'll leave when he arrives."

"I'd like you to go over it one more time. Please"

"I was trying to work it out. It's still a bit blurry. I met Clive at the diner. We left there and took our separate cars to The Grab Bar. We needed our own cars because we drive to work that way. Neither of us wanted to have to go back to the plant to get their car. So we got there, I suppose it was around 9:00."

"Nine o'clock?"

"Around there. I got there first. No, he was there first. I couldn't find him at first. It's really loud, crowded. We had a drink. I think he had two. I had one. A wine spritzer. We were chatting and one thing led to another and we started making out. But Clive kept interrupting and looking around and saying someone was watching us."

"Someone you never saw."

"Diane! Please!"

"He got this strange look on his face. His eyes kind of squinted and he pushed me away. He said someone was watching and he was going home. He got in his car and drove away. I got in my car and drove away. I thought someone was following me and it freaked me out, but that driver passed me on the highway. I took Old Weller because no one takes that road. But there was a driver coming at me and he blinded me and ran me off the road. Then there was someone and they were gone. And then someone else, and then fire fighters and an ambulance and here I am."

"What about the knife?"

I felt my face drop. Knife? No one said anything about a knife.

"I…"

"We are going to check your car's GPS."

I blinked and shook my head. What was going on with these two? Things had changed. Diane smirked.

"I don't have GPS."

"Your car does. Maybe you didn't realize it but–"

"I realized it. I disabled it. Rather, I took it to the shop and they disabled it."

"When?"

I looked at Diane. "Maybe three years ago?"

"Why?"

"Honestly...I used to be in a relationship with someone who valued their privacy."

"So you disabled the GPS?"

"My car and my phone. I have no trackers, no location, no data. I often turn my phone off when I drive." Diane and I had been incredibly cautious about being tracked together. It didn't matter most of the time, but at night, or days off, it did. She wanted nothing that would show anyone, ever, to connect us as lovers. Friends, sure. But not overnight. Not on vacation.

"What if you miss a phone call?"

"I do have voicemail."

"Can we get back to the knife please?"

"But I don't understand. What knife?"

"There was a knife found in your car."

I shook my head and looked at Diane. She shrugged. "You think I stole a knife from work?"

"Did you?"

"Why would I steal a knife from work?"

"You didn't answer the question. Let's be procedural until we know more about this knife. You are not under arrest. But we are questioning you." When Detective Scott started reading out the Miranda rights, Diane and I said them with him. It was something we always did when we watched TV shows. When the warning was given, we said it in unison.

"So...?"

"What was the question? Did I steal a knife? I'm a little lost."

"Tell me about the knife in the car."

I wondered at this point if police can lie to you. I think they can. I'm not under arrest, so they can probably lie all they want. "I don't have a knife in my car."

"We found a knife in your car."

"What kind of knife?"

"Was it a butter knife? I guess I might have had a butter knife in my car. But not from work. I'd have bought it. Though I don't know why it would be in my car."

Detective Scott rubbed his eyes. He was getting tired too. "A hunting knife."

"A hunting knife? Why would I have a hunting knife?"

"Ruby, please stop answering questions with questions. We're trying to figure out why you would have a hunting knife. Asking us what we're asking you, is not helpful."

Well, she had me there. This was not helpful at all.

"I had no hunting knife in my car. I don't own a hunting knife. I have never owned a hunting knife. That's one of those big spiky things, right? No. Don't own one. How's that for a direct answer?"

Detective Francine smiled. "That was perfect. You don't own and have never owned a hunting knife. But do you know how a hunting knife got into your car?"

I shook my head and looked at Diane. She looked right back at me. Useless.

"Maybe when I crashed, it was, like, on the road and it flipped up and landed inside my car."

"That's not very plausible."

"Well, I don't know physics very well. Maybe it is plausible. Are my fingerprints on it?"

The Detectives looked at each other and Diane rolled her eyes. Should I have not asked that question?

"Can we get your fingerprints, to compare to any we find on the knife?"

"You really should have a lawyer, Ruby." Diane finally said something useful.

"I haven't done anything, I don't need a lawyer. Should I give them my fingerprints? You're the medicolegal expert."

Diane shot me a look, but said nothing.

"Sure, take my prints."

Detective Scott grabbed his phone and stepped out. "We'll have a technician bring a portable fingerprint scanner for you. So you don't even have to come down to the station. We can do it here."

"But how would...Wait a second. That angel. No, not an angel. I know that. It was a man, I think."

As soon as I said that, Detective Francine sat up and leaned over, putting her hand on my bed. "A man?"

"Yes. He, I think he had a beard. He was...Diane, how tall are you?"

"Five foot four." I knew that.

"Maybe about five four, maybe five five. I think he had a flashlight and–"

Detective Scott walked back in and sat down. "What did I miss?"

"Ruby was telling me about a man. Five feet, four inches tall. The angel."

"Right. He had a flashlight and he shone it in my eyes so I couldn't see him. I think it was a man. It was really bright."

I held up my hand to silence myself while I thought. "He said something. A word or two. He...smashed the glass and said something and walked away. He didn't help me at all. He was no angel, that's for sure."

"Maybe he dropped the knife in her car?"

I think if the technician hadn't walked in at that moment, Detective Scott would have smacked Diane.

CHAPTER 8

"Diane, I'm not sure you're helping." I was trying to be polite, that was always best with Diane. The Detectives left the room. The technician entered the room, his blue uniform a stark contrast to the sterile white hospital walls. With a gentle touch, he placed my fingers and thumbs on the handheld scanner, capturing every ridge and loop of my fingerprints. The cold metal of the device sent shivers up my spine as it whirred to life, recording my unique patterns in perfect detail. Every swirl and curve seemed to tell a story, one that only I could understand. It was a surreal experience, having such an intimate part of myself captured and cataloged by a machine. It was nothing like the black ink process I'd seen on television.

For whatever reason, I couldn't shake off the feeling that this was somehow important, that these prints would hold some sort of weight in my future. And so I watched, mesmerized, as the technician completed his task with precision and efficiency.

It was like everything the Detectives were doing was designed to intimidate me.

"Ruby, baby, you know I'm here for you. Always."

"I don't understand what all of this has to do with anything. I mean, I had a car crash. I'm in the hospital. And those Detectives. Well, I'm getting confused."

Diane held my hand and smiled. "I got you, boo." She looked over her shoulder and upon seeing no one, continued. "I've been thinking. Maybe it was stupid for me to leave you. I really hurt you, I know that. But seeing you here, in the hospital? I guess it's putting my priorities straight. Would you take me back?"

I stared at Diane, my heart racing. I couldn't believe what I was hearing. After all the lies and betrayal, she still wanted to be with me? A part of me wanted to leap at the opportunity to be with her again, but my mind was telling me to be cautious. I couldn't open myself up to that again.

"Diane, I don't know. I need time to think about this. I don't know if this is the right time."

"It sure is, baby. I mean, take all the time you need. But please know that I'm here for you, no matter what."

I nodded and closed my eyes, trying to process everything that was happening. It was all so overwhelming. The crash, the Detectives, and now Diane's offer. My head was spinning, and a part of me wanted to escape it all.

As I lay there, lost in thought, I felt Diane's lips on mine. It was a gentle kiss, but it sent shivers down my spine.

"I know you're not ready, but I want you. I want to make things right between us."

"I don't think anything can put this right. The Detectives asked me about a knife. What do you think is going on?"

"Did someone attack you? Are there any knife wounds?" She started looking under my blanket, at my body, to find any bandages. There were none. "Did...Did Clive attack you? With a knife?"

I shook my head. "No, I...I don't think so. Why would Detectives treat me like this if he attacked me?"

"You're right. Why the hell would they? You know, I don't like this. I don't like any of this. They say there's no connection, and then take your fingerprints and read you your rights. But they leave all the time and...Well, I've had about enough of this crap!" There was that tone in her voice. The angry-as-hell voice. I could see the fury in her face. Her eyes went black and her nose crinkled and her cheeks turned red. Instead of yelling at me, Diane rushed out the door and into the hallway. I could hear her screaming at the Detectives.

"How dare you?"

I sat there, stunned. Even though I couldn't make out every word, I could tell from the volume of her voice that she was ripping them a new one. I couldn't blame her. They had treated me like a suspect, even though I was the one who had been attacked. I don't remember being attacked by a knife, though.

After a few minutes, Diane returned to the room, slamming the door shut behind her. I doubted the hospital workers liked that. She looked like she wanted to say something, but instead, she stormed over to the window and stared outside.

The sky was painted with a blend of fiery oranges and soft purples, signaling the approaching nightfall. I love purple, have I told you that? Probably not. I like it because it's the color of shadows before they turn black and rotten. But they were purple, adding to the peaceful atmosphere.

"Diane, are you okay?"

She turned to face me, her eyes still brimming with anger. "No, I'm not okay. Those people accused you of something you didn't do."

"What exactly have they accused me of?"

"I have no idea. They aren't even saying what they think you've done. They are so vague. They're doing terrible work. They're supposed to be finding the person who attacked you, not making you feel like a criminal. I can't believe this is happening."

I nodded, not really sure what to say. It's like it was happening to her, when really it was happening to me. There was a part of me that was grateful for Diane's outburst. It showed that she cared about me and wasn't going to let anyone treat me unfairly. But at the same time, I didn't want her to get me into trouble for yelling at the Detectives.

I leaned back against the bed and closed my eyes, trying to remember every detail of the night in question. But no matter how hard I tried, I couldn't make sense of it all.

"Honey?" I didn't open my eyes at the sound of her voice. "Baby, let me take care of this for you. Let me be your...your assistant. Like a lawyer. I can tell you which questions to answer and which to avoid. I know these types of Detectives. I work with them all the time. They're bullies. They purposefully make things vague and confusing. Let me make it right for you."

I have to hand it to her, Diane can sound very sincere at times. I drew in a deep breath. "What if they ask you to leave? What if they arrest me? Charge me with, I don't know. I don't even know." I admit I was getting more emotional than I expected.

"We'll find out together. Okay?"

"Okay."

"Okay. I'll get the Detectives." And with that, she got up and got the Detectives.

When they walked back in, Diane first, she was pleased. There was a big smile on her face and she said, "The Detectives see it my way. I'll stay here with you."

"Okay Ruby, we need to talk about the knife."

"I've said, I don't know anything about a knife. And I have you my fingerprints. There is no way on God's green earth my fingerprints are on a knife."

"Can I show you a picture of the knife? It's a little dirty, but maybe you'll recognize it."

I nodded and Detective Scott got up to show me a photo on his phone. There it was. The knife. I know something about hunting knives. This was a Bowie knife. A wide blade, 10 to 12 inches long with a clipped point. It had a cross guard to protect the user's hand. It would have been beautiful except it had blood on it.

"I've never seen the knife before."

"Diane? Have you ever seen the knife before?"

"Me? No, of course not. Let me see it again? No. I was...I was at a crime scene, last year, where there was a knife. Not like this, a kitchen knife."

"To be clear, you haven't seen this knife?"

"Never in my life."

"Okay, alright. Let's put that aside and talk about the blood."

CHAPTER 9

"What blood?"

"There was blood in your car."

"Well, I was in an accident. I guess I bled."

Detective Francine shook her head. "Your bruises are from blunt force. The bleeding you did was very minor."

"Very."

"Then what?"

Detective Scott showed me another photograph. It was blood. A pool of blood that was in my car. I recognize the tear in the head rest.

"Okay?" I didn't know what else to say.

"What can you tell me about the blood?"

"I guess it's my blood. I bled more than you realize. You aren't doctors, after all." I was getting testy again. This was going on far too long. I wanted a lawyer, because it seemed to be serious, but I didn't want a lawyer, because then I'd look guilty.

"It's on the passenger seat."

"Huh?" I hadn't been listening.

"Look, you weren't in the passenger seat. How did the blood get there?"

"I...I don't know. I don't know anything about a knife. I don't know anything about the blood. I don't know anything about being run off the road. I don't know how it connects. I–"

"Wait, can I take a look? I'm a medicolegal death investigator, after all."

"Sure. Take a look."

"This? This blood here? It's on the passenger side seat back."

"Passenger side, that's right."

"But look at the angle." Diane turned the phone, but the picture flipped and she turned it back. "Do you have other photographs? A good investigator would have photos from multiple angles."

Detective Scott grunted and took the phone back. He flipped through a few more images, and held it up for Diane to see.

"There! See the direction of the blood flow? Someone has poured this blood into the car, while it was on an angle. Was the car on an angle baby?"

She let 'baby' slip again, and the Detectives both raised their eyebrows. I ignored it. "The car was on an angle, yes. Tilted, um, passenger side down."

"There. Check the records from Rescue Services. They'll confirm if the car was passenger side down."

Detective Francine smiled a little. "We'll have to have our own blood spatter expert evaluate the blood flow."

"And that hasn't happened yet?"

"Not yet." I wonder if the Detectives would tell us if it had. Do the police have to tell you everything when they interview you? I'm trying to think back to TV shows. They always do in fictional shows. Show the evidence to the suspect, that is. They pull out guns and papers and maps and bloody clothes. Very dramatic.

But in real life interviews? I don't think so. Yes, I think Detectives can withhold information if they want.

"Well you tell whoever it is, they need to analyze the angled blood flow."

"What does all this mean? Where did the blood come from?" I was still pretty confused. Not listening doesn't help.

"It means someone poured blood in your car."

"It could mean that. It could mean other things."

"Why would anyone pour blood in my car?"

"You said earlier, something about feeling wet? Do you recall that?"

I laid back, trying to think. "Yes. I remember...no, I remember something wet. When the man with the beard showed up. Do you think he poured blood on me?"

Diane brushed a bit of hair from my eyes, though I hadn't even noticed it. Everything seemed to be getting out of control, and I had to think. And think I did. Out loud, for the Detectives to hear.

"So hang on. Hang on. I go out with Clive for a drink, someone is watching us. Someone follows me when I leave, then...catches up to me in the opposite direction? Runs me off the road. Tries to...stab me with a knife, but drops it. And pours blood on me. No wait! Maybe they cut themselves on the knife by accident, and the blood poured out and they dropped the knife and ran away. Drove away. That sounds pretty possible to me."

"You're forgetting one important piece of the puzzle."

"Clive is dead."

"Did someone run him off the road too? Oh my God! Did someone run us both off the road?" I sat up, eyes wide, staring at the Detectives.

"No. That's not how Clive died."

"How'd he die?"

"Exsanguination."

I know I blinked a lot at that word. I know what it means. Clive bled to death. But what did that–

"No. No no no. No way! You think I killed Clive! No no no no no. You're wrong. You think I stabbed Clive, don't you? With that big hunting knife!" I started shaking so badly that Diane had to hold my hands.

"They aren't saying that. Are you saying that?"

"Ruby, did you kill Clive Benning?"

"No! No no! I liked Clive. He was a nice guy. I know what people said about him, but he was a nice guy to me."

Diane gave me a funny look, and I remembered she hadn't heard me when I said Clive and I kissed. Or did she? I don't know anymore.

"I didn't kill anyone. Not Clive, no one. That's horrible."

"It is horrible. It's a horrible crime scene."

"If he was stabbed, by that hunting knife, the scene would be covered in blood."

"It is."

"And there would be blood on the perpetrator most likely. Fingerprints in blood, blood on clothing. There would be blood on everything."

"You're right Diane, there would be a lot of blood on things. Ruby, can we look at your clothes?"

"I'm not wearing any clothes. I have a hospital gown on."

"I mean the ones under your bed. In the plastic bag."

"I was in an accident. Of course there would be blood on my clothes."

"You didn't really bleed a lot from the accident."

"Then it's what was poured on me. Maybe that guy poured blood on me?"

"The one who drove you off the road?"

"Yes!"

Detective Francine gave a sideways glance to Detective Scott.

"Okay. If you were crashed in your car, tilted with the passenger side down, and someone poured blood on you, there would be almost no spatter. I know these things, I've been to a lot of crime scenes. Pours don't result in a lot of spatter. Is the blood on Ruby's clothes spatter? Or a stream?"

"We can't discuss that directly. Ruby, are those your shoes?"

"I don't know, I can't see what you're pointing at."

Detective Scott got up and reached under my hospital bed. In a clear plastic bag were my shoes. Clean, white shoes. No blood, at least not to the naked eye. "Size eight?" He was looking at the size tag, what a stupid question to ask.

"Yes, I wear a size eight."

"Does it matter what her shoe–oh! You have footprints in blood at the crime scene! You can look at the bottom of her shoes. Look at the bottom. Is there blood?"

Detective Scott turned over the shoes, and there was no blood. "They're very clean. Are they new?"

"No. I mean, maybe a month old. But I keep my shoes clean, you know?"

"Eight."

"Huh?"

Detective Francine wasn't talking to me, she was talking to Detective Scott. He repeated the word, "Eight," and put the shoes back under my bed. He stayed down a little longer than expected, but soon enough popped his head up. I bet he looked at my clothes while he was down there.

"Size eight."

"Your so-called expert should be able to tell you the shoe type." Diane didn't win any friends with that comment.

"We know the shoe type. Brand and size."

"Well then?"

"Well what? You think we should skip over questions and not do our work properly? That's not how we work. We are thorough. Very thorough."

I started to cry. I didn't mean to, it kind of came out. The stress was so much. I was tired and shaking and crying. I was grateful when the Detectives left. I hope I never see them again.

Chapter 10

Diane was so sweet to me while I cried. I don't think Detectives should be allowed to talk to you when you're emotional. Diane gave me tissues and a glass of fresh water. I think I am done with the police.

And…They're back.

"Can you tell me what happened?" I needed to know.

As soon as a crocodile smile appeared on Detective Scott's face, I regretted asking that question. It was big and toothy but there was no warmth to it. They weren't teeth at all, but a whole muzzle. A muzzle ready to tear me apart.

"Clive Benning was found dead this morning in his home. A couple of painters had arrived to do some work, and found him. Early estimate is, he died sometime late last night or the early morning. From stab wounds from a large knife with a serrated edge. The wounds generally match the hunting knife found in your car. Your car, Ruby."

"No no no! I didn't kill Clive! I swear! Oh my God. Diane, make it stop, please!" I didn't want this again. It was a nightmare.

In response, Diane held up her hand. "Who are the painters? Maybe they killed him."

"And planted the knife?"

"You have to consider it."

"Ruby, do you know this man?" Detective Scott showed me a photograph of a red-eyed man with shaggy brown hair and a beard and mustache. I shook my head. He showed me another photo. A blond, with short spiky hair.

"No. I don't know them."

"They are the painters who found Clive. Called it in."

"So they could have killed Clive. It's not unheard of for the 911 caller to be the killer." I'd never heard that before, but Diane would know better than me.

"There was no blood on their coveralls."

"They could have changed. Did you check their van?"

"Of course we did! We're Detectives." Detective Francine was now the one to lose her cool.

"But they would have killed him last night, then pretended to find him this morning. That's plenty of time to change."

"Why would painters kill Clive?" I knew it was a naïve question, but I had to ask.

"Robbery. I've seen it before. Break into his house–"

"There were no signs of break-in."

"How did the painters find him?"

"They had a key."

"Well, there you go. Use the key when he's away. Rob him, but he comes home. Stab him. Then plant the knife on Ruby."

"How would they have known about Ruby?"

"Oh! The person watching us?"

"Yes! One painter watching Clive and...watching you? Anyway, one painter watching and one painter robbing. Then they kill Clive, follow Ruby, run her off the road and frame her."

"No. The timeline is wrong."

"How do you know the timeline?"

"If Ruby and Clive left the bar at the same time, the painters would have to have followed her from the bar to know who she was."

"No no. One painter at the bar, one at the house. Bar painter calls house painter, says Clive is on his way home. House painter tells bar painter to follow Ruby and plant evidence on her."

"If they knew Benning was coming home, why wouldn't they leave? Instead of killing him? How did bar painter get the knife ahead of the crime? Call up his mother and ask her to deliver it?"

Diane fell silent. Maybe I shouldn't have asked that question, mentioned Diane's mom, but it shut Diane up, so it was worth it.

"Look, I can't explain the knife in my car. I really can't. Maybe a painter ran me off the road and then returned with the weapon. If it's in my car, it will have my DNA. But it won't have my fingerprints because I never touched it."

"You need to search the painters' van."

"We know what we're doing, Diane. Ruby, how tall are you?"

"Five foot eight. One hundred and thirty pounds, give or take."

"I'm five foot four." I don't think Diane needed to say that, but she really needs to be the center of attention. She didn't give her weight as she had always been self-conscious of her size.

"Blue!" I shouted it out the moment I remembered it. "The car that charged me was blue. Not black. It was blue. I remember that more."

"Blue car. Okay, think about the blue car."

"I saw the lights and I screamed and I turned the wheel. There was a loud scraping noise. I guess that's when I hit the pole."

"Scraping sound?"

"Yes. I think I scraped the car. I think he got so close I actually scraped against the car."

"You scraped the car that night? In the accident?"

"Yes. When else would I have done it? My car was fine that morning."

"Maybe it scraped against the pole."

"No no, I'd have missed the pole then. I hit the pole. I scraped the car and hit the pole. I'm certain of it now."

"Then you Detectives can get samples of the paint from her car, right? It will at least give you a make and model."

"What is your make and model?"

"Cayson Shock."

"Mine's an Amery Falcon." I shot her a look. She knows that's not actually her car.

Detective Francine shook her head sightly at Diane's response. "Let's park that and get back to Clive."

"That poor man."

"You knew him, right?"

I hesitated in front of Diane, but had to agree. "Yes, I knew him from work."

"And the bar."

"Yes, of course. The Grab Bar."

"How well did you know him?"

"Not well. Mostly from gossip at work."

"One of my colleagues has had a chance to speak with Steven Cartwright. Do you know Steven?"

"No, who is he?"

"Clive's best friend. He knows who you are."

My heart about leaped out of my throat. "I've never heard of Steven."

"Steven and Clive were in touch the night Clive died."

Damn! Why hadn't I thought of that? "Yes?"

"That's when Steven heard your name. Or saw your name, at any rate. Text messages. Clive texted Steven. The message said...'Ruby from work. She's sad. LOL. Peach. Eggplant. Waterdrops.'"

It meant Clive texted Steven and told him about me. "Well yes, I said I saw Clive at the bar."

"When we spoke with Steven, he told us a little about Clive."

"Clive was a player. And he had a type. He liked to find women who were sad or upset, and be sympathetic. He'd give her a shoulder to cry on, then take her home."

"I didn't go home with him. I left the bar and went home and crashed."

"There's evidence of someone being there with him. At the house. In his bedroom."

I almost threw up. "It wasn't me."

"Okay stop asking those questions. Ruby isn't that type of woman."

"What type of woman are you, Ruby?" Detective Francine said my name, but she was staring at Diane. "Who's your type?"

"Okay, can I have Ruby alone please?" Thank God for Dr. Galliano. He scooted everyone out and sat down by my bed.

"Ruby, I know you are in a very stressful situation. I don't exactly know why the police are so interested in you. But my concern is your medical condition."

"Give it to me straight, doctor. I can take it." I felt like one of those old fashioned romance novel heroines who's about to be told she has consumption.

Dr. Galliano laughed. "You have only minor damage. You must have been driving quite slow. The Detectives have not asked me that, and if they do, they will need a warrant for your medical information. You are fine. We will be releasing you tomorrow. And that, I will tell the Detectives. Do you understand what I am saying?"

I understood him alright. The Detectives think I killed Clive and this might be my last night on the right side of prison bars.

"Yes doctor, thank you."

CHAPTER 11

Dr. Galliano left and the nurse arrived. She checked numbers and calibrated dials. She wasn't friendly to me anymore. She must think I'm a killer.

"I'm not, you know."

She didn't take the bait, she didn't ask me what I meant. She looked at me briefly, made one more change, and walked out. I had been mistaken. She wasn't a nurse I knew. There are so many of them, coming in and out, checking this and that.

I watched as the nurse shut the door behind her, leaving me alone in the hospital room. Alone again... I started to sing that old song in my mind. You know the one? The machines surrounding me beeped and whirred, their mechanical symphony filling the awkward silence. I couldn't help but feel a sense of unease settle over me.

Despite my attempts to convince myself otherwise, doubt gnawed at the corners of my mind. What if I truly was a killer? And I didn't remember? It seems like something you'd remember.

I spent the next ten minutes thinking about what to say to the Detectives. They are supposed to prove your guilt, but really, I had to prove my innocence. I knew I ought to tell the whole truth, for my own sake. But it would only make me look guiltier. Was that even a word? It should be.

Diane walked into the room and interrupted my thoughts. She brought two coffees, apparently both for herself. "The cops have stepped outside. Ruby, baby, please tell me what's really going on. I know you. I know when you're lying."

Diane was looking very earnestly into my eyes. It was the same look she had before telling me she was leaving me for her secretary. I saw a shadow pass by the frosted glass between my room and the hallway. It was probably the Detectives. But if it was, they didn't walk in.

"The Detectives think I killed Clive. That I stabbed him and drove off with the knife. They think I killed a man."

"You're right baby, I think they think that. But I don't. I know you better than they do. It's not like you're a cold blooded killer who goes around stabbing people because they annoy you."

"Diane...that knife."

"Look, I've been thinking. This could all be a set-up."

"Could be?"

"Is. Is a set-up. Someone wants to kill Clive. There are two ways: try to hide what you've done, or frame someone else. They're framing you. Someone ran you off the road to plant evidence. Maybe they hoped you'd die and that would be the end of it. But you didn't die."

"But how?"

"Easy. I looked to where Clive Benning lives. He is literally three miles from your home. I checked the distance. Because you live in the middle of nowhere, you have to take the highway from the bar. That's the common route. But Clive's home is in town. My map shows Clive lives two miles from the bar. You live twelve miles. There's an unnamed road that cuts across a field, avoiding the highway. If you take that road, Clive's house is three miles from his front door to yours. It's absolutely possible that someone killed Clive, drove that road, and drove at you to run you off the road. Then, you said someone came by. That's the driver, planting evidence."

I took a shaky breath. "Why me?"

"Maybe the killer was fleeing the scene, and you unluckily happened to be in the wrong place at the wrong time.

Maybe you were targeted. The real killer puts the knife in your car and–"

"Why not put my prints on the knife?"

"Because then your prints would be above the dried blood. The real killer would have left fingerprints under or in the blood. It would have been an obvious plant."

"And the blood on the car?"

"It was poured. I swear, they should check the crash area for a bloody cup. I..." Diane trailed off and smiled. She held her finger to her lips as a gesture of silence, and walked over to one of the Detectives' chairs. Detective Scott had left his phone behind. Diane picked it up, swiped and almost shouted with excitement when it opened.

"Oh my God, Diane! What are you doing?" My eyes turned to the door, terrified we'd get caught.

"No. No. Trust me. There. He left the photo app open. I'm looking at crime scene photos. He only has a few. Sent by his death investigator, no doubt. Body, body. Gruesome overkill. Shirt. Wall. There! I knew it. Drag marks through the blood."

"The killer dragged him?"

"No. The marks are too small. More like a cup scooping up blood."

"They scooped the blood and poured it in my car with the knife? Diane, this is sounding more and more outrageous. Who would ever have thought this up? It's diabol-ical."

"You heard the Detectives. He took advantage of women, they said so. If you make the wrong woman angry, she will burn the world down to get you."

"Who will?"

Detectives Francine and Scott walked in with coffee. No one offered me a coffee. Diane stood stock still, Detective Scott's phone in her hand. He snatched it angrily out of her hand.

"You're interfering with the investigation."

"I have a theory."

"I don't care."

"No, let's hear her out."

Diane laid out her theory. Clive slept with a married woman, her husband found out. The husband followed Clive until they ended up in Clive's house. The husband murdered Clive in a fit of rage, maybe they even argued. Husband comes up with an idea to set someone up. He takes the knife and some blood, runs a stranger off the road, plants the evidence, and voila!

"That's quite a theory. You're missing some key points, though."

"Like what?"

"Like the damage to the car."

"He ran her off the road, Damaging her car."

"Your problem is, you don't have all the information. All the evidence. So you concoct these crazy theories based on nothing."

"That's harsh."

"What about the painters?"

Detective Francine had a big smile. "They've been arrested for theft from Clive Benning's house."

"That's not murder."

"Diane, stop."

"Look, Ruby. We'd like to speak to you tomorrow. Maybe at the station?"

"I guess so. If they release me."

"I'll leave my card. Give me a call." And the Detectives walked out.

Diane flopped down in the chair, her hands on her head. "I was right to begin with. The painters. The painters, baby. You're in the clear."

"That was terrifying. Is that what always happens in police interviews? Hours and hours of questions?"

"Not always. They were grasping at straws. Them, not me. I said the painters to begin with."

"Did you? You did. You were right."

"Baby, I'm sorry about everything. Everything I've done."

I looked at Diane. She had no idea what she'd done to me, how she'd hurt me. And here she was, apologizing.

"It's been a lot, today."

"You're right. It has. I'll prove myself to you. I still love you. I'll show you." She kissed me on the cheek and held my hand and spent an hour talking about all the ways she'd make up breaking my heart. She fiddled with my bed settings, moved the IV, and lowered the lights. The nurse finally chased her out. I am so tired, and this has been too much. A car crash, a murder, an accusation and an offer of reconciliation. I feel like I'm in some twisted romance movie.

I am finally alone. Everyone left their garbage behind, and since I'm not bed-bound, I thought I'd clean up. I grabbed hold of my IV stand, got out of bed, and gathered everything up. Why can't people clean up after themselves. This is a hospital. It's supposed to be sterile. The cleaner had left a bottle of cleaner, so I used it. Now I was really tired, and it took all my energy to get back into bed.

CHAPTER 12

I had fallen asleep. Very quickly. I had no idea until I heard the nurse shouting my name and hurting my chest. I managed to open my eyes and the nurse stopped her torturous rubbing. Two nurses and a doctor I'd never seen were fussing over me. I had an oxygen mask on. Now what?

"Ruby, can you hear me?"

"Yesh."

"How are you feeling?"

"A little fuzzy."

"Do you know what happened?" I shook my head. I had no idea what was going on. I got a new IV and a few needles of things, and eventually things were less fuzzy.

"Do you know what happened?" It was my turn to ask.

"We aren't sure. You had an episode. We don't know why. You'll be sent for a CT, and we'll go from there."

"Am I okay?" *What the heck is an 'episode'?*

"We're going to move you to another room, Ruby. Closer to the nursing station. It will be a little easier to make sure you're okay."

"Okay."

They wheeled me through the bright hallway and into a room across the hall from the nursing station. I fell into an uneasy sleep. The night nurse woke me up to take me for an x-ray. I fell asleep again, only to be woken again by the day nurse. The sun was out, and she kindly opened the drapes and propped my pillow up behind my head after raising me into a sitting position. Dr. Galliano was back. He had the Detectives with him, and I almost cried.

I don't understand why they won't leave me alone. I'm pretty sure I didn't kill Clive. No, let me restate that. I am absolutely certain I didn't kill Clive. I was beginning to hate both the Detectives. Even Francine, who seemed nice.

"Ruby, I've asked the Detectives to speak with you about last night." He walked out, leaving me with Detectives Scott and Francine.

"Hi."

"Hi Ruby. How are you feeling?"

"Okay I guess."

"Did you know what happened last night?"

"No?"

"What do you remember?"

Ah, this game again. "You left. Diane left. I fell asleep. The nurse woke me up and said I'd had a seizure."

"Did you eat or drink anything?"

"No."

"The doctor is concerned you might have tried to hurt yourself."

I laughed. "I think the world is already handling that quite well, thank you." How absurd.

"You didn't try to hurt yourself?"

"No. I didn't try to hurt myself. I didn't–" Diane walked in with a coffee. "I didn't hurt Clive. I didn't hurt anyone."

"You two start early, don't you? Why the room change?" Diane walked in as pretty as you please. She had on a soft pink lipstick. My favorite. And a little eyeshadow. She once told me what the color was. 'Evening Glory' or 'Temptation Tonight' or something that doesn't actually tell you what the color is.

"To be near the nursing station. I don't think they are releasing me today."

"Let's shut the door so we have a little privacy. You're still okay to talk to us?"

"Yes."

"We had a chance to talk more with the painters. They did rob Clive's house. We have them for that. But they have solid alibis for the evening when Clive died."

I nodded. "So you're back to me, then?" The damned heart monitor started going up, and there was no way to pull off the sticky without being seen.

"We have a statement from Cliff's neighbor, a guy who was getting home from work at 10:45 p.m. He saw someone leave Clive's house. A woman."

The monitors were telling my story. Heart rate up, blood pressure up. Beep beep beep. The damned beeps.

"Ruby. They described a person about five foot five, and about one hundred and thirty pounds. Sound familiar?"

I began shaking. They knew! They knew and my life as I knew it was about to end.

"Ruby?"

I held up my hands, hoping to stop their words. I couldn't look at Diane. I wanted to vomit.

"Clive and I were dating." I could see Diane's face twist. Her eyes went black and she sneered. She looked like an animal that wanted to rip my throat out. "I didn't see him after we went to the bar. Not that night. But we were dating."

Diane slammed the foot bar of my bed and stormed out. There is nothing I can do about it now.

"So you were at his home that night, and…"

"No. I wasn't. I was there the night before. You check with your eye witness. You'll find out the date is wrong. I'd–" Diane walked back in. "– been over a few times. You'll find my DNA somewhere I'm sure. But he had a thing about cleaning, so I have no idea how much."

"A thing about cleaning?"

"Yes. God, yes. He'd clean everything. That guy would wash the dishes right after using them. Clive would even vacuum while I was still there. He scrubbed the toilet bowl after a…number two."

"No one has mentioned that."

"Oh you ask his best friend, he'll tell you."

"Have you met his best friend?"

"No. Clive never talked about anyone in his life. He kept it on a need to know basis. I never met his mother, either, but he spoke about her a little."

"So you've been to Clive's house?"

"Yes. I told you. Look, have you talked to the neighbor on the left? Clive told me he was having a problem with them."

"Neighbors on the left? What kind of problem?"

I can't believe where this is going. These Detectives want to know every little detail. And Diane is ready to explode. Again.

"There was a dispute over the property line. Something about their recycling box always being on Clive's side of the property? He told me they almost came to blows about it."

"Why are you mentioning this now? Why not earlier when I asked if you knew anyone Clive was feuding with?"

I couldn't stand the sight of Detective Scott anymore, so I looked out the window. "It's embarrassing. Dating Clive is embarrassing. I hate to speak ill of the dead, but he was a dummy. Not to me, but he was an idiot to a lot of people. Not enough for someone to kill him. Not unless that person was really unhinged. But he ticked a lot of people off. His idea of a nice dinner was a diner attached to a gas station. And I had to pay my own way. He wasn't exactly Mr. Suave."

"Is there anything else you should be telling us?"

"Should be? Well, I shouldn't be telling you anything. I should be at home with a nice glass of wine and a little music on, reading a good book. Even a terrible book. But I certainly shouldn't be lying in a hospital bed talking to Detectives about my boyfriend's murder."

Diane sat down. She'd been gripping the bed frame like a vice, but now she flopped down into the chair.

"Boyfriend?"

"It's only a word, it didn't get that far. We were..."

"Did you have sex?"

I quickly looked at Diane, but she had turned ashen and had her eyes closed.

"Not full-on sex, no. But we fooled around."

"Necking?" I didn't like the tone in Detective Scott's voice. It seemed condescending.

"Yes."

"Who else knew about the two of you?"

"No one. No one that I know of, anyway. I don't know what Clive told anyone. You'd have to ask around."

A nurse came in, thankfully, and asked everyone to leave while she took my vitals. She said my heart rate was elevated, and by blood pressure was a little high. Yeah, no kidding. I'd told two Detectives that I'd been dating a man, right in front of the closeted ex-girlfriend who wanted to get back together with me. If that isn't worthy of high blood pressure, I don't know what is.

CHAPTER 13

Diane was the first one back in the room, and she was furious. She started to whisper yell at me.

"Who the hell do you think you are? You never told me about this. I mean, what the hell, Ruby? Clive? Are you serious?"

"Diane, hear me out–"

"No! I don't want to hear a damn thing. You lied to me even worse than before. You were with him while I wanted to fix things."

"I didn't know you wanted to fix anything. You were sleeping with your secretary for God's sake!"

"You're unbelievable. I thought we had something worth saving. But you're a liar, Ruby. A damn liar!"

"Diane, Clive was only a friend. Nothing happened between us."

"Save it! I trusted you. I opened my heart to you, and this is how you repay me? Sneaking around with some guy? You destroyed us, Ruby. You threw away everything we had, and for what? Some fling with Clive? Or were you going to live together or something? I guess not now. Not if he's dead. I can't believe I wanted you back. I can't believe I wanted us back! You dated him and he died. Horribly. Maybe there's a lesson to be learned."

"A lesson to be learned? What does that mean? Why are you being so mean to me?" I thought I was immune to her anger, but I was wrong. Diane's words stung terribly. I started crying, I didn't know what else to do.

"You can turn off the fake tears, you two-timer! I know they're fake. You never cared about me, did you?"

I looked up, and through teary eyes, could see how red her face was, how spittle flew from her mouth as she spoke. I turned away.

"Don't you–"

"Is everything okay in here?" Once again, the Detectives came to the rescue.

"Fine."

What else was Diane going to say? That she was so filled with malicious rage that she wanted to throttle me?

"Diane, you seem to be taking Ruby's relationship with Clive quite personally."

"I am not."

"Yes, you are."

"Look, Ruby is a little...naïve. I said it before. She doesn't know what she gets herself into sometimes."

"What's it to you though?"

"We're best friends."

"Is there more to your relationship?"

"Of course not." Diane said that with practiced conviction.

"You've always been such a good liar. Yes! Yes Diane and I were in a relationship. She broke it off to be with her secretary, and now she wants back with me. I should have listened to your mother and left you a long time ago."

Diane almost leaped onto the bed. "You take that back. She doesn't know what she's saying. She's on medication, she's saying silly things."

"If one of you will get me my phone, I can prove it."

Diane froze. It felt good to see the fear in her eyes. Detective Francine handed me my phone. I unlocked it, went to my photos, and started scrolling. Diane almost threw up when I handed over the phone.

"There. Lots of pictures of us together. Check the dates. The photos–"

"We were best friends! Of course we have photos together. We did a lot of things together, had a lot of fun.

Ruby, why are you twisting this into something unnatural?" The pleading in her eyes was the only thing unnatural here.

"Detectives, she's the reason I have no GPS in my car, no way to track my phone. She insisted no one ever know about us. Ever. She told me how to turn off all those features. To turn off the phone when I was out with her. She's the one who–"

Diane lunged for me, but Detective Scott held her back. As soon as he touched her, she shrank back.

"Scott?" Detective Francine motioned for Detective Scott to take a look at a photo in my phone. I tried to see which one it was, but couldn't make it out. She whispered in his ear. I wanted to scold her for whispering, but that hardly seemed appropriate.

Detective Scott looked at the photograph, at me, and then at Diane. "Diane, can I speak to you outside?"

Well, that's hardly something you can say no to, is it? So Detective Scott and Diane headed outside, while Detective Francine sat in a chair beside me. She still had my phone.

"How long were you two together?"

It was scary talking about this. I couldn't talk to anyone before. "Three years, more or less."

"Three years. Did she always yell like this?"

"It's not really yelling, is it? She used to say that. She isn't yelling, she's talking forcefully. Not always. But sometimes. She can be envious. Even though we aren't together, even though she is the one who left me. I don't think that matters. I think that once you were hers, you were always going to be hers. You know, I used to think it was kind of romantic. All this secrecy and intensity. I mean, almost like we were sneaking around. In fact, we were sneaking around. If word got out that she likes women, she'd probably lose her investigator position. Although, dating the secretary is probably not too discreet, hmm?"

"Did she ever hit you? Or hurt you?"

"Not really. Nothing I went to see a doctor about."

"Did she ever threaten you? Threaten to hurt you for any reason?"

I sighed and looked to the ceiling for answers. Those ceiling tiles were still silent. "Diane is complicated. She likes to be the center of attention, she likes to be in control. You've noticed that, I'm sure." I heard the heart rate monitor start beeping faster. I wish I could turn the damned thing off. "She loses her temper a little. Not much. Not often."

"So no doctor visits?"

"No. I did call the police once. Shortly after we broke up. You can check the records."

"Tell me about that."

"She came over to my house, pretty angry, and we got into a fight. It got, I don't know, a little scary I guess. I called police. They showed up but by then, Diane was back to her old self. Very sophisticated, you know? You've seen how she can be. She told the police it was mostly my fault, that I called them to get her into trouble. I didn't…I didn't really say anything. I mean, what could I say? She was being mean to me? That's childish. So I didn't say much of anything. And the police officers kind of got angry for wasting their time and they left. I didn't get their names or anything. Police officers in uniform."

"Did they make a report?"

"If they did, they didn't tell me about it. No one called back or anything like that."

"What will Diane say about this incident?"

I had to laugh at that one. "Who knows? That I hit her? That it never even happened? That I dreamed it? She, she, what's that word? She lights me?"

"Gaslight?"

"Is that it? Where someone makes you think something didn't happen?"

"Yes."

"Yes. Gaslight. She's very good at gaslighting."

"What happened after that?"

"After we broke up? Not much. She didn't reach out or see how I was or anything. I was...Honestly, I was pretty devastated. It had been three years before she dumped me. I guess I was...lonely. I guess that's where Clive comes into the picture. Like you said, he can lend a sympathetic ear."

"But you didn't sleep together?"

"No. I wasn't ready for that yet."

"And you were together on the night he died?"

I nodded. It was the best I could do.

"And you were sad and lonely, but you ended up going home alone?"

"Yes, because Clive was getting paranoid."

"About someone following him. And then you left."

"And someone followed me, but then went away."

"And then someone drove you off the road and came over to you, but didn't help. Right?"

"That's right. The person didn't help me."

Detective Francine leaned back in her chair and stared at my phone.

CHAPTER 14

Detective Francine left me for a moment then came back with Detective Scott and Diane and everyone sat down. The atmosphere seemed different, somehow.

"Diane, can you explain this photograph to us?"

Diane took my phone and looked at the photo. I couldn't tell which one it was, but her face softened when she looked at it. "Two besties going on vacay."

That sounded hollow, and fake.

"Where did you vacation?"

"Aruba. December, last year."

"Two rooms?"

Diane paused. She'd thought having two rooms wasn't necessary–Aruba seemed so far away–so we booked a single room. "One room. But two beds. We're friends."

"I understand. Was Aruba nice?"

"Oh, it was beautiful. So warm. Friendly people, too."

"Yes. That's a lovely photograph of the two of you smiling. That...that's a nice top. Did you buy it there?"

"Umm, yes, the blue number. It is beautiful, very affordable there."

"What about your shirt, Ruby? In this photograph?"

They finally showed me the photo they were looking at. I was in a plain white shirt with short sleeves. Diane was in a blue linen shirt with a small heart embroidered on it. "I brought my shirt with me, I didn't buy any clothes there."

"Do you two ever swap tops?"

"We're quite different sizes. In case you hadn't noticed, Detective." Diane seemed outraged at the thought that I might wear her clothing. That hurt me. But she was right. We were very different body shapes.

"Why are you lying to us?"

I looked up, and was incredibly relieved to see they were looking at Diane, not me. She, on the other hand, looked shocked.

"Lying? I'm not lying." She flicked her eyes in my direction, but I'd already told the truth and there was no going back.

"Ruby says you were together for three years."

"Three– Oh Ruby, why? Why did you have to tell them?" It was heartening to see Diane almost crying. "Yes, so what? We were together for three years. But you don't know what it's like around here. I could lose my position, lose my pension. Please, don't tell anyone."

"You can't lose anything, Diane, that's against the law. And actually, I do know what it's like. I'm gay, but I'm out and no one cares."

Well, you could have floored me. I'd have guessed Detective Francine before I guessed Detective Scott. He didn't look gay, if that makes sense. I did not pick up on a single vibe.

"No, not for me. For me, it's different. I get that maybe you don't have to be discreet, but I do."

"There's discreet, and there's secretive."

"So what? So what if I was secretive? It's my secret to keep."

"Hers too. It's Ruby's secret too, to live like that."

"So what? Who cares? We broke up and now..."

Diane paused and drew a deep breath. I knew something was coming, I didn't know what it was.

"We broke up and Ruby started to date a guy and if you ask me, she killed him. There! I said it! I'm not protecting you anymore. I know exactly how it happened. And if you Detectives haven't figured it out yet, shame on you."

"Diane!" I want to say I was shocked by her accusation, but I wasn't. I knew she thought it was me all along. That's her way.

"I'm the medicolegal death investigator here. I'm the crime scene expert. I saw those photos, I heard the stories. I've been here from the start, I heard everything. Ruby met Clive at a bar, went to his home and for whatever reasons, killed him. Then she took the knife and some blood–maybe to drink later, I don't know."

I almost threw up at those words.

"She got careless and crashed her car on the way home. I bet there was no other car. There was no person to set you up with a knife. What a ridiculous story. The pour pattern is from where your cup of blood splashed. Ruby, you're sick, you're a sick woman."

I am sitting quietly, listening, until she finishes. I don't know how to defend myself against these accusations.

"I...I..." Nothing would come out.

"Ruby, did you have some coffee, yesterday?"

"No. I had the water. All of you had coffee, you even had two, Diane. But no one offered me any."

The Detectives looked at each other, and Detective Scott started filming with his camera.

"Diane, did you have two coffees yesterday?"

"Yes, I suppose so. What of it? Is it a crime now not to give a treacherous woman a coffee?"

"Ruby, did you drink her coffee?"

"I don't understand. She gave me a sip, but I didn't like it."

"I did not!"

"You did too. A sip though, it was too bitter. I've never been one for coffee."

"You're lying. Why are you lying about coffee?"

"Diane, did you know about Clive?"

"What? Of course not."

"Where were you Wednesday night?"

"Oh no. No way. Don't you dare come for me."

"Answer the question or we'll arrest you right now."

"You can't arrest me. I can't have an arrest record, or the medical examiner's office will fire me. I can't be arrested."

"So if there was a disturbance at your home, and the police were called, you wouldn't want to be arrested?"

"Of course not, who would?"

"Not charged, mind you, but arrested."

"Arrested, that's the rule. You can't be arrested. Clean living is vital."

"Where were you Wednesday night into Thursday morning?"

Diane paused and shot me a look that could have sliced through me. "At home. Alone."

"Can you prove it? Did you call anyone or..."

"No. No I was asleep."

"Does your car have GPS?"

"No. And not my phone, either. Untraceable. Like Ruby."

"Diane Emerat, you have th–"

"No! No way!"

Diane leaped to her feet and tried to run out of the room. All I could do was watch as the Detectives got out of her way and let her open the hospital room door. Three uniformed officers were standing on the other side. Diane wheeled about in very dramatic form, much like a leading lady in an old noir murder mystery film.

Despite her protests, Diane sat back down and was read her rights. I've never seen anyone arrested before and I have to say, it's exciting.

"Yes I understand my rights. But you have no evidence. None! I didn't do it! I didn't kill Clive."

"The paint on Ruby's car? You recommended we test it, remember? To find the make and model. It's a factory paint coating on an Amery Falcon. That's your car, isn't it?"

"Wait, wait, wait." I didn't know what else to say. "You really think she did it?"

My heart rate monitor started to beep so fast, the nurse rushed in. She took a quick look around, turned the monitor off, and left.

Detective Scott laughed a little. "And we think she tried to kill you, too."

"I fucking did not!"

I was shocked, I don't think I'd ever heard that kind of language from Diane. But once she got started, she kept going with it.

"You fucking twits! I haven't done anything. She isn't even worth trying to kill!"

"Hey!" I mean, that's very hurtful, isn't it?

I laid back and covered my face with my hands. This was so much to take in.

"Aargh!" Diane was shouting as she tried to ram my bed. I don't know what that would have gotten her, but the Detectives and police in uniform stopped her. There was a scuffle, and a few more swear words, and the police officers lead her away.

After some reassurances from the Detectives that I would be safe now, and some reassurances from me that I would testify, they left.

They finally left.

CHAPTER 15

It's been a week since I was poisoned with cleaning fluid, and the doctors have said I can go. There would be no lasting effects. I'm grateful for that.

The sterile odor of the hospital still lingers in my nostrils, a constant reminder of the invisible enemy that once danced through my veins. The echo of the grim reaper's whisper still causes goosebumps to pepper my skin. I wonder why hospitals need to smell like this. Why can't cleaners smell like, I don't know, strawberries? I guess people would drink the cleaners then, and maybe not even know it. At least I knew it.

The nurse is insisting I use a wheelchair until I get out the door of the hospital. "Safety protocols." I don't mind. It's a rainy day, and I am happy to sit here alone and wait for my cab. It's a bit chilly, I don't really have much in the way of clothing.

Detectives Francine and Scott have come back twice since they arrested Diane. Detective Francine said they saw it from the beginning: Diane inserting herself into the investigation. She was trying to direct the Detectives away from her, toward me. Diane set me up, and then tried to poison me. She never actually said that Diane set me up for Clive's murder, but I know that's what the Detectives think.

I have to admit, the whole thing was really clever.

The rain is coming down a little harder, and I'm grateful for the overhang protecting me from the elements. The hospital has a lot of grass, and people are stepping into the mud to get past me. No one is asking me to move. They'd rather walk around the woman in the wheelchair than ask her to move. That's okay, it's their shoes that are getting dirty, not mine.

My shoes are clean. Of course. I didn't wear my shoes when I killed Clive. I'd bought a pair of size six shoes, the same kind Diane wears, at a thrift store. I basically had to walk on my tiptoes in those things, to stop my heels from making an impression.

Thanks Diane, you helped me set you up in ways you will never know.

One thing Diane always complained about when we watched murder mysteries was, when the killer wore larger shoes to hide his foot size. A larger size doesn't exclude you, but a smaller size? Well, most Detectives don't think that way.

And it's true. My Detectives didn't think that way. They suspected me, then they suspected the painters, then me, then Diane. That was sweet when they finally twigged. I think it was drinking that damned cleaner that finally sealed the deal. 'Oh no Detective, I'd never try to kill myself.' Ha! I didn't, either. I knew a little would make me sick, not kill me. I put on a pair of gloves–there are a lot around a hospital–and poured myself a little cleaner in one of Diane's used cups. I'm grateful to the nurse who got suspicious, and kept the garbage from the room. Or maybe the Detectives told her to. Either way, it incriminates Diane while my fingerprints won't be found on the cleaner.

The hair had been easy to plant. The shirt too. Diane had left it at my house when she broke up with me. I don't think she meant to, but it was pretty symbolic. You know, 'we had a great vacation together in Aruba and I'm leaving that behind.' The photos were pretty easy to handle, too. I uploaded everything to the cloud, then deleted most of the images. I left enough for the Detectives to browse through and see the one where she was wearing the same shirt.

I probably should have left the knife at Clive's and ended it there, but I'd decided to frame myself barely enough to make it look like Diane had framed me.

Diane was such a braggart about being a medicolegal death investigator. She taught me a lot about crime scenes and evidence handling. Fool.

Clive and I left the bar separately and met up at his place. No one was watching us, no one was following us. But I said he said that, to put it into the Detectives' minds that maybe it was Diane who was spying on us. Funny.

When I got to his place, I parked around the corner, put on some gloves, and brought the knife and a change of clothes with me. I'd bought that at the thrift shop, too. Now, that one could come back to bite me, but let's hope not.

Stabbing Clive was really easy. Stabby, stabby. Kidney first, from behind. He was dead in seconds, never made a sound. Then the subclavian artery, running into the heart. Thanks again to Diane for the ideas. She was always full of ways to kill someone quickly. I didn't want Clive to suffer even though he was a nobody to me.

Diane had told me once that killers always leave some kind of signature. I doubt that, but I used it. I saw that Clive had a bunch of red plastic cups, so I scooped up some blood and took it with me. I wasn't sure at the time what I'd do with it.

Now, it really could have been anyone I met at The Grab Bar that night. That I knew Clive from work, well that worked out quite sweetly. I concocted the idea of a relationship to make Diane look even more envious. Sometimes, a plan really comes together.

I was mad from the day we broke up. I thought, I'll get you for this. Making me live in secret for years, and then leaving me for a goddamn secretary.

Driving into her car was nerve wracking. I wanted to…I guess I wanted to kill myself by smashing my car into hers. But I chickened out at the last minute, and swerved. The cars scraped, but that's it. I drove off and parked my car in my garage and didn't drive it again until that day.

It was serendipitous, really. I crashed that night, and evidence would look like Diane had run me off the road. And she even told me she knew a short cut from Clive's home! I delighted in telling Detective Francine that sweet little piece of information. I wonder if they can check the map app on her phone. Probably.

So I drove along the highway, onto Old Weller, and when no one was around, I poured blood down the back of the passenger seat and threw the cup out of the window, put the knife on the seat on top of the blood, and drove into the pole. It took forever for someone to come along and help me. I mean, I fell asleep while I waited. But finally someone came, and called for an ambulance, and here I sit. Waiting for a cab to take me home, while Diane sits in prison wondering what the hell happened.

I'm sure she'll say that I set her up. I mean, the blouse and the hair could only have come from her or me. But as long as the police think it's her, with all the other evidence, it doesn't look good for her.

You know, if she'd only been nicer to me, none of this would have happened. But she isn't a nice person. She's a mean person. Like when she thought Clive and I were a thing. Woo! That was some great envy for the Detectives to see. That was motive, right there. I had no motive to kill Clive. But Diane had means, motive and, since she can't prove where she was, opportunity. The trifecta of my freedom.

FRANCINE

CHAPTER 16

As the sun began to rise, its rays crept between the tall buildings and cast a warm glow on the city streets. We arrived at the scene, our presence announced with a loud siren wailing through the air. The vibrant colors of the sky contrasted against the dull gray of the concrete masses, creating an otherworldly atmosphere. Our arrival was met with curious gazes from passersby, as we quickly assessed the situation and prepared to take action.

"Detective Temple."

"Detective O'Reilly. What can you tell us?"

Scotty loved saying that. He grew up watching some old forensic science TV show where the lead Detective would always ask, 'what can you tell me?' I thought it was cute, in a geeky sort of way. Police tape surrounded the house we stood in front of, and Forensic staff–real Forensic staff–were busy as bees all over the place.

"I'm Officer Suskind. We have one Clive Benning, deceased. Looks like two defects. One to the kidney, one to the upper chest. Lots of blood. Found by two painters who'd arrived to do the living room. They are over there."

We turned to where Suskind pointed. Standing by a police cruiser were two men in white painter coveralls. Spotless white painter coveralls. "The tall one is Diego Garcia, and the short one is Miguel Sanchez."

"Let's hear what they have to say."

"I'll take Sanchez."

Scotty and I strode confidently towards the two men, their tense postures giving away their nerves. Garcia towered over us at 6'5", his wide frame filling the space around him. Despite Suskind's comment, Sanchez was not short, but rather stood at a sturdy 6 feet tall. As we approached, I couldn't help but feel a slight sense of intimidation from Garcia's imposing figure.

"Mr. Sanchez? I hear you found Mr. Benning?"

"Yes ma'am. Our company sent us out to paint the living room here, and when we got here, we hadca key and unlocked the door. I figured he was expecting us, and walked in. I mean, I knocked, but he...he was lying there in the hallway with lots of blood. I called 911."

"When did you arrive?"

"7:50 this morning. We start at 8 a.m., but it's always a good idea to arrive a little early, you know?" As Sanchez spoke, I noticed his hands trembling and his eyes darting around nervously. He seemed genuinely shaken by the discovery of the body.

"Did you notice anything unusual when you arrived?"

"No, nothing out of the ordinary."

"We were about to head inside when we saw him on the floor. We didn't touch anything, we swear."

I glanced at Scotty, who was busy with Garcia. "Can you describe Mr. Benning? Did you know him personally?"

"No, we've only painted for him once before. He was a quiet guy, kept to himself mostly."

"And you didn't touch anything inside?"

"Uh, I knocked on the door, maybe touched the door handle. Um, maybe the wall. I think I might have touched the wall trying to get past Garcia. It really freaked me out. I had to run, you know?"

"I understand. But you didn't go into the kitchen or living room or any other place than the hall?"

"No, ma'am."

"Okay. I'm going to have an Officer take you and your buddy downtown for formal statements. Okay?"

"I can drive us," he said, pointing to his van. It was a standard issue white van with the words "Salvadore's Painting LLC" on the side. Unfortunately, the back door of the van was closed, so we wouldn't be able to look inside.

"No, sorry. It's part of the crime scene now. You can call your boss from the precinct, tell him to contact Homicide Department. They'll give him information on how to get his van."

"What do you mean, 'part of the crime scene'? We did nothing." He got panicky a little too quickly.

"I'm not saying you did. But suppose the killer left tire tracks out here. And your van tires get into the mix. We need to take an impression of the tire tracks on your van to make sure we rule them out. It's pretty straightforward stuff."

"Uh, okay, yeah." Well of course 'yeah,' you don't have a choice. I escorted Sanchez to the cruiser as Scotty was finishing up his interview. Garcia was put into a separate cruiser and they took both men downtown.

"I called ahead. Someone will take their statement."

"Thanks. Hey! We need Forensics to take tire impressions on the van!" I shouted as I pointed to the van. A tech raised his hand and gave me a thumbs up.

"Shall we?" Scotty and I walked into the house.

The victim lay in the doorway of the bedroom, half in the room and half in the hallway. He was face down, a bloody wound obvious on his back. Another pool of blood was around his head and chest. There were shoe prints leading from the body through the kitchen out the back door. The techs pointed out some blood splatter on the walls.

"No signs of forced entry?"

"No sir. We have found some long blonde hair in the blood, and there was a blouse shoved into the corner. There was what appeared to be blood on it. That's been collected."

"Excellent, thanks."

Scotty and I walked outside. The sun was brighter. It looked like it was going to be a beautiful day. "Detectives? A woman in that blue house said she saw something last night."

We headed over to the faded light blue house. An older woman stood on the porch, her arms crossed over her chest.

"Hello ma'am. I'm Detective O'Reilly. This is Detective Temple."

"I'm Edith Kaiser."

"Hi Edith, what did you see?"

Edith crossed her arms tighter before speaking. "I saw someone ou' his back yard las' nigh'. I don' sleep well, so I si' on my back porch. I saw someone, don' know who. Didn' see a face though."

"Do you know what time that was?"

"Around, maybe 1:30 or so."

"Okay, thank y–"

"They walked funny, though. With a limp in both legs."

"Okay, thank you. Here's my card. Please call if you think of something else."

We sent a few officers around the neighborhood to look for door cam footage and we were about to head to the office when I got a call.

"Detective Temple."

"Detective, this is Officer Andrews, Traffic Services. I'm on Old Weller Road at the scene of a single vehicle accident. There is a large knife inside the car with what appeared to be blood on it. I was told by paramedics the victim didn't have any such cut wounds on her. There is a lot of blood in the car. My partner, Officer Pritchard, is at the hospital with the driver."

Andrews should have called the Homicide Department, but I know him, so I guess he thought calling me directly was okay.

"And aside from the knife and blood, what's got your attention?"

"Well, if there was a passenger who's been harmed? I haven't seen anything on site yet, but I think it's worth a look."

Andrews was a trustworthy guy. "Yep. We're not far away. O'Reilly and I will head over. Secure the scene."

There were only four Homicide Detectives in Little Bluff, and we were the only two awake. "Scotty, great luck. We might have another case. Old Weller Road."

Scotty and I headed over in our separate cars. I used my GPS system, and it recommended a shortcut via an old dirt road. I was glad for it, even though it made my car a little dirtier than normal. It shaved about twenty minutes of the roundabout route but didn't do the suspension any favors.

The road cut through a cornfield. The amber waves looked stunning. Before I knew it, I was at Old Weller Road. I turned west, Scotty following behind me, as we drove to the scene.

We both parked on the side of the road and walked up to Officer Andrews, introducing ourselves and shaking hands.

"Thanks for coming, Detectives."

"No worries. What's up?"

"Well, first of, the knife. A large Bowie knife sitting there, and all that blood." He pointed to a knife covered in blood. On the passenger seat was a pool of blood down the back of the seat. It's the kind of thing you might see if the passenger's neck was slashed. The passenger side door was shut but the window open.

"I'm doing accident reconstruction, but initially, it looks like a slow speed impact. My partner, Pritchard, is at the hospital with the driver.

"What's the driver's name?"

"Ruby Fisher. She was unconscious. It's Little Bluff Hospital. Pritchard is with her."

"What about this?" Scotty pointed to the damage to the side of the car.

"That's probably two, maybe three weeks old."

"Alright. I'll need Pritchard's phone number. Can you give me the driver's information?"

I took a photograph of Ruby Fisher's registration card, and Scotty and I headed to the hospital. I was hoping we could wrap up this little mystery quickly so we could get back to the real murder.

"Get a rush DNA on the knife and the blood."

"Yes ma'am."

"Alright Scotty, ready?"

Chapter 17

On the drive to the hospital, I sent a message to Officer Pritchard to let him know we were on our way, and wanted an update from him. Scotty pulled his car up beside mine and honked repeatedly. I rolled my eyes and put my phone down. He gave me a thumbs up and sped off. Goof.

Little Bluff Hospital is the regional hospital for the area. What it lacks in sophistication, it more than makes up in generalization. Chopped your foot off in a farming accident? They can reattach it. Overdosing on meth? They can bring you back. But if you have leukemia or congenital heart disease, you have a long drive ahead of you to a better hospital.

Scotty and I pull into the parking lot. There are plenty of spaces. Although everyone here drives, the size of the parking lot is massive.

"Twenty-five bucks for parking? That's robbery."

"Go arrest the doctor."

"Ooh, a comedian."

"There's Pritchard." We head over to Officer Pritchard, who has been waiting patiently for us by the entrance.

"Ruby Fisher. Thirty-five year old white female. Have you been to the crash site?"

"Yes."

"Then you know, it wasn't that bad. By my rough field calculations, she was going maybe 10 miles an hour when she hit the tree. I know Old Weller Road. Most people are doing 50 or 60 down that road. Fisher appears disoriented, and a little hostile. Her doctor is Dr. Galliano. And she works at Peachtree Fabrication. That's all she has told me so far."

We thanked Pritchard and headed in to talk to Dr. Galliano. He will tell us a little, but not much, about Ruby's condition. I hope she's cleared to be interviewed. I'm a little miffed that we're even here. I'd much rather be working on the Benning case.

"Detectives O'Reilly and Temple, Little Bluff Police. Can you locate Dr. Galliano for us please?"

"Yes, please have a seat, he will be a moment."

We sat down at a couple of seats nowhere near any-one. "What have we got on Benning?" Scotty and I were scrolling through text messages and photographs from the techs at the scene, and the techs in the lab.

"Clive Benning, 38, white male, two stab wounds. Right kidney and right subclavian vein."

"Subclavian?"

"It's the big ziti in your chest."

"Are you hungry?"

"Yeah, a little. Why?"

"Maybe you should eat before you get hangry."

"I don't get hangry."

"You do."

"Don't."

"You're hangry right now."

"Maybe you're–"

Dr. Galliano emerged from a back room and greeted us. He was a tall, thin man with graying hair and a kind smile.

"Detectives, how can I help you?" Scotty and I stood up and shook his hand, introducing ourselves.

"We're here to get an update on Ruby Fisher's condition and to see if she's able to be interviewed. We'd like to speak to her, the driver in a car accident. We'd like your medical clearance, and any information you feel comfortable in providing, including any toxicology, sir." Such a diplomat, my Scotty.

"Yes, Ms. Fisher is conscious and stable. She suffered a concussion and some bruising from the airbag, but nothing significant. Ms. Fisher is currently awake and alert, which is a positive sign. However, I must inform you that she is experiencing confusion, likely due to the traumatic nature of the incident. We're monitoring her closely, and she might not be able to provide a clear account of the events at this time. In terms of her bruises and wounds, they are relatively minor. She has some external abrasions and contusions, but nothing severe. We've conducted thorough scans, including CT scans and x-rays, and they reveal no internal damage or fractures. It appears that the primary impact was external, and she's quite fortunate in that regard."

"Did you test for alcohol or drugs?"

"Yes, the tests were negative, she was not impaired. Now, considering her current state of confusion, I would recommend approaching any questioning with sensitivity. The mental trauma from the accident might affect her ability to recall events accurately. I believe she can be interviewed, but it should be done with care to avoid causing undue stress. We are prioritizing Ms. Fisher's health, and I appreciate your understanding in that matter. If there's anything else medically related that you need to know, please feel free to ask."

We thanked Dr. Galliano and sat back down. I was getting information on the crash, and Scotty was getting information on the murder. Andrews at the car crash scene sent a text. 'Initial analysis: vehicle left road approx 30 ft before pole. Tire tracks on dirt shoulder. There's trash at the entry point. To be collected. Note no skid marks or brake indications on the dirt shoulder, suggest no attempt to slow down.'

"Scotty, check this out. The driver didn't try to slow down before she hit the post."

"But not impaired. Tired? Distracted? On purpose?"

"Maybe. There are scratches and dents from an earlier accident. Maybe she likes driving into things. Like in that movie."

"That Cronenberg film? You're a nut. Maybe it's Munchausen Syndrome. Wanting to be the center of attention?"

"Nah, you'd have the accident where people would actually find you. Do we know when she crashed?"

"Nope."

"And we still don't know what the knife was about."

"Maybe she was going to slash her wrists, but then decided to crash her car. Maybe she stabbed Clive Benning and was trying to get away and crashed. Maybe there was another person in the car to explain everything."

"Okay, let's go talk to Ms. Fisher."

We found Ruby Fisher in Room 7B, knocked, and walked inside. She was asleep in the hospital bed.

"Ruby Fisher?"

She snorted awake and was immediately a little spicy with us. We introduced ourselves and asked her about the accident. She was an odd duck. She'd start talking and then fade away, like she was thinking. Maybe it was accident PTSD or whatever the doctor had suggested.

"It was cold. Probably. I don't exactly remember the last few days so clearly. But yes, the windows would have been rolled up."

She was very focused on the windows, so I texted Andrews and asked if the windows were up or down.

'Driver up. Passenger down.'

"Where were you going?"

"Where did I crash?"

"Old Weller Road."

"Ah! I was either coming or going. I live on Yurton Road. Off Old Weller."

"128 Yurton?"

"Oh yes. You know that?"

"It's on your car registration. So were you coming or going?"

Ruby got a little testy with Scotty, which I thought was hilarious. He was usually a woman's favorite. Scotty and I looked at each other and I nodded: he was to be the bad cop, I was to be the good cop.

"You were driving eastbound on Old Weller when your car went off the road. You went into a ditch and tipped the car."

One of the monitors started to beep, and a nurse came scurrying in. She replaced the IV bag, fiddled with a few settings, and snapped at us: "Detectives is this really necessary?"

"Yes ma'am. We'll try to be quick."

Ruby was an inquisitive woman, always eager to ask the same questions over and over. She had a knack for getting under your skin. I think she likes making others uncomfortable. So when she came right out and asked what had happened, I wasn't surprised. As a seasoned homicide Detective with 10 years of experience on the force, I was used to knowing when someone was trying to deceive us. Even my partner Scotty, who had been with Little Bluff police for almost as long as I have, could sense when someone was trying to pull the wool over our eyes. But Ruby's directness was refreshing and I couldn't help but admire her tenacity in seeking the truth.

CHAPTER 18

Scotty and I want to get the hell out of there. We want to get back to the real work. Scotty got a text from the techs at the crime scene.

'Strands long blonde hair.'

We looked at each other, then at Ruby. She had short black hair. Not dyed. They weren't her hairs. I looked back at Scotty with a pleading, 'can we go now?' look.

Before either of us could move, the door banged open and a woman walked in. A woman with long blonde hair. There was something obnoxious about her, something that drew all eyes to her as if she were the source of a strange smell in the room. Like something rotten.

"Ba-Ruby? Ruby, what happened?"

The woman rushed over to Ruby's bedside. I looked at Scotty and mouthed, 'baby?' She asked us who we are.

"Detectives O'Reilly and Temple. Who are you?"

"Diane Emerat. Ruby's friend. The hospital called. Ruby, what happened? They said you were in an accident."

I made note of Diane's name. Lots of things are going through my head now. A car crash not far from a murder scene, long blonde hair at the crime scene, and now a blonde with long hair has walked in. I'm a cop. I hate coincidence. Everything changed.

"The Detectives were telling me there was an accident, but I don't remember to well."

"Is she under arrest?"

"No. Should she be?" Scotty was channeling his inner Bogart with that beauty.

"No, I... Sorry. Sorry about that. Let me start again. I'm Diane Emerat. I'm a medicolegal death investigator in Peterson County. I've heard of you both, Detectives. Homicide, aren't you?"

"We are."

I texted the office. 'Diane Emerat, a medicolegal death investigator in Peterson County. Did she help at our crime scene? Check with P.County.'

In moments of crisis, those in service to their community go above and beyond. A cop, a fire fighter, they don't hesitate or shy away because of arbitrary boundaries. It's in their nature to put others before themselves. I'd never heard of crime scene techs crossing into another county's territory, but in this situation anything was possible.

"Was someone else hurt?"

"Stop. Would you mind if we chat? The two of us?"

"Who are you to her?"

"We're best friends. I've known Ruby for years."

"Is that why the hospital called?"

"Yes. I'm still your emergency contact. You really scared me."

"I'm really scared."

"I'd like a few minutes. To check in. Between besties. Please."

"We'll get coffee. Either of you want anything from the hospital cafeteria?"

"No, neither of us. Thank you."

Scotty and I headed out to the cafeteria.

"No way are they only 'besties.' Five bucks says they are exes."

"I'll take that. I say they are currently together."

The sterile hospital cafeteria was a dimly lit sanctuary for the exhausted and worried. Plastic chairs lined up in rows, their backs curved from years of use, and tables wobbled on uneven legs. The scent of stale coffee mingled with the antiseptic smell of cleaners, creating an oddly comforting aroma. Doctors and nurses sat slumped in their seats, their tired eyes betraying the long hours they had spent saving lives. Terrified family members huddled together at tables, seeking solace in each other's presence. We purchased two cups of coffee and took a seat at a nearby table, our voices hushed to avoid disturbing the heavy atmosphere. Each person around us was lost in their own tragedy, creating a sense of isolation despite being surrounded by others.

"Do you think this is connected with Clive Benning?"

"I don't know. Something weird is going on. The coincidences are too much."

"God this coffee is horrible." And it was. Stale, cool and flavored like the inside of the paper cup. My phone buzzed and I looked at the message.

"Damn Scotty. We have our first twist. Diane Emerat is a data entry clerk with the Peterson County coroner's office. Not a death investigator."

"What a strange lie. I mean, she must know we'd check."

"Not if she thinks she's smart and we're stupid. What do you want to do about it?"

"Find out more about them. I think we need the DNA from the knife and the blood. At least the preliminary that will tell us male or female. If it's male, we'll get a search warrant for Fisher's car and house."

"Sounds good. Should I be heading over to the Benning place to–"

"Oh no you don't. You're staying right here with me mister. Let's get back."

"Meanie. I want to push on the car accident a little. Say we think two cars were involved, maybe she was run off the road. Let's see how she runs with it."

"I don't know, it sounds kind of fishy, doesn't it?"

"Fishy, Fisher, it's all the same."

"Goof."

We headed back to Fisher's room. "Ladies, I hope we aren't interrupting?"

"No, not at all." Diane then repeated her claim that she was a death investigator.

"Ruby, it looks like there might have been a second car involved. The crime scene technician said there was damage to your car along the side. Do you know about damage to your car?"

Ruby said nothing, but anyone could see the wheels in her head spinning. Then she finally spoke.

"When was all this again?"

A thought nagged at me, like a persistent itch that I couldn't scratch. Was she truly experiencing these memory lapses or was it all an act? Doubt crept in, leaving me with an uneasy feeling in the pit of my stomach. Her expressions seemed rehearsed, her words carefully chosen. It was as if she were putting on a show for my benefit. Our benefit. But why? She was genuinely in a car crash. A small part of me couldn't shake off the possibility that it all might be a facade.

"We think it was late Wednesday night or early Thursday morning. You were found by a man on his way to his work. He called for an ambulance."

"I was there all night?"

Scotty signaled me that he got a text message, so I drew attention to myself. "Do you remember it now?"

"What was the last thing you remember?" Diane asked the question, surprising Scotty and me.

Scotty pulled more information from Ruby while I sent him a quick text. 'Diane is insinuating herself into invest.'

Ruby said she worked at Peachtree Fabrications, a local company. Scotty turned to his phone while I kept going. "And you remember working on Wednesday? At Peachtree Fabrications?"

Ruby hesitated. Why would she hesitate? She ought to know if she was at work that day. I got a text from Scotty. 'Benning worked Peachtree'.

No coincidences. I thought I'd push her a bit more. "Did you go out for a drink with your co-workers?"

When I asked, Diane laughed. I wondered if they'd been together at the crash, if Diane had been in the passenger seat.

"No. I'd have gone straight home. I...I'm quite certain I made myself a pasta salad. Yes. I distinctly remember grating the Parmesan. Parmigiano-Reggiano, the real stuff."

"Okay, so you were at work, and you went home and had dinner. Were you alone?" Diane was hovering over Ruby when she answered, and then chastised us for asking, suggesting we stop the questions.

"Ms. Emerat, please let us do our work. We don't want to upset Ruby." The woman was up to something. Lying, distracting, interfering.

"Ruby? Did you have a dinner guest?"

"No. I am certain I ate alone."

"You ate alone, and you didn't go out that evening with co-workers for a drink? Not before or after dinner?"

"Do you ever hang out with co-workers? Maybe not that night, but any time?" Scotty was trying to find out if she'd ever gone out with Benning. If she denied it and we proved it later, it would be yet another red flag lie. Both of them seemed untrustworthy.

"Not really."

"Do you and Diane have dinner together sometimes?"

"Sometimes, yes, that's what best friends do."

CHAPTER 19

Ruby was doing her level best not to answer most of our questions. Her face twisted into a mask of apprehension as she tightly pursed her lips, refusing to answer, guessing, humming and hawing. Her eyes darted back and forth, avoiding direct contact with anyone in the room. It was clear that she was conflicted - either she truly didn't know the answer, or she had ulterior motives for remaining silent. Killing someone will do that to people sometimes.

Maybe, and this is what I think, she wants to be able to say to a defense lawyer that we'd told her, not that she told us. We had to tread carefully. And of course, Diane didn't help.

"I don't like these questions. They are too open ended."

"Ma'am, you're here because we allow it. Please don't interrupt." Scotty was snippy with her. My phone buzzed in my hand. 'DNA on knife, blood same. Male.' I got so excited I kind of glitched in my chair. To cover my yip, I got up and threw my coffee out.

Time to ask. "Do you know Clive Benning?"

"No. Did he run me off the road?"

"No. He works at Peachtree too. A coworker."

"I don't know Clive Benning. Clive was not at my home for dinner. Ever."

Ruby looked terrified when she realized we knew they worked for the same company. Beads of sweat formed on her brow. The air around us seemed to thicken with tension, making it hard to breathe as we waited for her next move.

"Did he run her off the road?" Scotty shot Diane a look. It was a good distraction. I texted the team. 'Warrants, Fisher, home & car. ASAP. Test knife DNA against Benning.' I didn't think we had enough to go after Diane. So far, she was nothing but annoying. She said nothing to give me any sense that she is involved, but damn! She grates on me more than Ruby.

I received a long email giving me information on Benning's employment. What a scumbag.

Ruby continued to deny knowing Benning, and Diane continued to ask questions. Scotty finally asked her to leave. She acquiesced and went for coffee.

"Okay. Let's try again. You don't work with Clive?"

"No. I really work with the sales team. They give me their orders, and I enter the orders into the system."

Ruby suggested we talk to the others in the office. What a great idea. Another text to the team: 'Talk to Peachtree sales office re Ruby and Clive.' Every question we asked about Clive was a denial she worked with or even knew him.

"Not with Clive?"

"No. Where did Clive work?"

"The floor. He's a machinist with Peachtree."

"Clive Benning worked for Peachtree Fabrications for three years. Three days ago, the company suspended him. Seems he harassed some of the other employees. Uh, hung a noose on the shop floor, drew a Hitler mustache on the photo of an employee of the month. Did you hear about any of this?"

Ruby shook her head. I'd hoped that without Diane in the room she'd be more talkative. Instead, she talked less.

"From what we understand, from talking with other people at Peachtree, he was a piece of work. Suspended first thing Monday morning. We spoke with Human Resources."

"Grace."

"Yes. Grace Horowitz. She told us he was suspended with cause. He was caught peeping into the women's washroom."

Ruby surprised me a little when she tried to cast doubt on Benning's bad behavior. It occurred to me briefly that maybe she had a head wound. But when the nurse walked in to take some vitals, I watched Ruby's face. She watched the woman like a hawk. No wavering, no loss of focus, no distraction. Nope. No head wound.

"Mr. Benning had been fired the previous year, but won his position back when the Union fought on his behalf. HR hadn't properly documented the complaints. But he seems to have been a guy who couldn't change his spots, as it were."

Ruby wasn't listening. I let it go.

"I'm sorry. I don't understand what Clive has to do with me?"

"We aren't sure he does. Nothing concrete."

"Nothing concrete? About what?" Diane was back.

"They have nothing concrete tying me to Clive."

"You didn't know him?"

"No."

"He's dead."

Scotty could be very blunt, but it worked. Ruby finally responded in a way that made it seem like she did, in fact, know him.

Lying in the hospital bed, Ruby's eyes remained fixed on the ceiling tiles above. Scotty's words hung in the air, and Ruby said nothing at all.

Suddenly, the monotonous beeping of the blood pressure monitor bucked and an alarm started to sound. Ruby sharply inhaled. Her hands trembled, clutching the thin hospital blanket.

The nurse, alerted by the relentless alarms, entered the room with a sense of urgency. She moved quickly, checking the monitors and addressing the blaring alarms. Ruby turned her attention to the nurse. She seemed to like to be saved by others. Good to know. Ruby finally asked the question we expected 20 minutes ago. "Did I hit him with my car?"

And then she lost it. She let out a loud wail. We tried to calm her down, but she got worse.

"Why would you scare us like that?"

Us? They sound like they are still a couple.

"We're trying–" Scotty's phone buzzed. He read the message before continuing. "Trying to find out what happened to him."

I'd told them that Benning died in his home, making sure I didn't say how he died.

"Oh! Oh! You think she might have seen something? That's it! Isn't it? Oh bab–Ruby, try to remember. Try hard to remember what happened that night." Good old Diane was once again trying to redirect the story.

"Oh for the love of God, woman! Please stop. One more time and you're out." Scotty was really losing his patience. He got up and walked out. I followed.

"Scotty, are you losing it?"

"Nope. Email from the coroner. The blonde hair belonged to a woman. There is a blouse." He turned his phone for me to see a blue top. "Not Benning's size. But one woman's top. No other women's clothing, so it doesn't look like it would belong to a regular girlfriend. There is blood on it, but not splatter. It looks like it was dipped in the blood."

"What the hell? Why?"

Scotty shook his head. "Some kind of weird ritual?"

"Did we ev–Dr. Galliano! Sir. Sorry I bother you, quick question. When Ms. Fisher came in, did she have blood on her?"

"I'm sorry Detective, I don't know. Not by the time I saw her."

"Okay, thank you." I turned back to Scotty and asked if he could follow up with the paramedics. He texted them before I texted Andrews.

"We can also check her clothing."

"Only if she gives us permission."

"Not ready to let her know she's a suspect yet."

"Then you will have to check it out through the plastic bag under the hospital bed."

"Yep. I can do that."

Scotty then gave me an update on the search of the car. Aside from the knife and the blood pool, they found a used wet wipe in her purse. It had what appeared to be blood on it. It was already being tested.

"Please let her DNA and his DNA be on the wet wipe."

There were a few other things of no interest. A purse with the standard fare: lipstick, sunglasses, old candy and a tampon. A phone charger.

"Oh! Oh! Oh!" Scotty got very excited and hustled me into a corner. He switched from a shout to a whisper. "They found long blonde hair in a hairbrush in her purse."

We high-fived each other. It wasn't everything, but it wasn't nothing. Scotty said the techs had found used but old condoms in the waste basket at Benning's There was a receipt for gas at a gas station and a receipt for a single drink at a bar on the night of his death. They were almost done processing the scene.

CHAPTER 20

I can't quite figure out Diane's part in this mess. Was she a passenger? Or maybe the driver of the car when it crashed. Then she gets out and moves Ruby over. No, no, that's too far-fetched. But Diane is mixed up in this somehow.

Scotty and I came up with a plan. We'd press Ruby for details in the hopes she'd contradict herself. We'd press Diane in the hopes of getting her to give us one more little thing to get a search warrant on her house. It wasn't much of a plan, but we still couldn't tell if it was one or both of them. We headed back in.

"Let's start all over again. Diane, please, don't talk. You can be here for support, but that's all. Okay?"

"Okay."

"Ruby, let's go over Wednesday night again. You need to tell us. You worked, you went home, you had supper alone. You remember all that."

"Yes."

"Then you went out. We know that because you said your car was pointing in the direction of home when you were found. Now, there was a 911 call from someone who saw your car. That was at 5:46 a.m. We need to know what happened between the time you finished dinner, and the time you were found."

Ruby paused at this, playing for time. Ruby said she'd had dinner at home, then went out.

"I live alone, you see."

"You were lonely, and you got into your car to go somewhere."

"Yes. I remember putting the radio on. Talk radio. I like to hear the voices. Hear someone talking."

"I live alone too. I get it." I was trying to show a little empathy. It was a lie–I live with my wife and our three kiddos–but she didn't need to know that.

"Where did you drive to?"

"I..."

"Yes?"

"I went to a bar." Ruby reached up and covered her mouth. She was a terrible actress. It reminded me of something you'd see in a 1920s film. I wondered if she was going to fake faint in a moment.

"Do you know which bar?"

"Did I crash because I was drunk?"

"No! No way! Not Ruby. You don't know her like I do. She'd never drive drunk. Not ever." Scotty was pissed Diane was interrupting again.

"No. Your blood alcohol level was negligible."

"I drove to The Grab Bar." I knew the place. The cheesy bar was a neon lit cavern of mismatched furniture and glitter-covered walls. It smelled of stale beer and piss. Loud music from the 2010s blared through crappy, residential speakers. It was a dingy little place at the edge of town.

"The Grab Bar?"

"That's it. Get out. Diane, out now. Go." Scotty pointed to the door. I took Diane's arm and stepped out into the hall.

"I have to apologize for my partner. I don't think he's showing you enough respect. I mean, you're a medi...what do you call it?"

"Medicolegal death investigator."

"Right. So you're aware that we have to cover everything. Figure out if she was out, was she drinking, who likely saw her, that kind of thing."

"What does this have to do with a dead man?"

"We aren't sure. The Grab Bar is notorious for assaults and even two homicides this year alone. I'm sure you've talked to death investigators in this county about it."

"Now that you mention it, yes. I do know The Grab Bar. In fact, I've been there, on an investigation. As a consultant, of course."

Her lying was bothering me. There was no reason for it. Unless, of course, she'd been lying to Ruby while they were together. Then Diane would definitely need to keep the facade going.

"So you see, we're trying to put pieces together so we can leave Ruby in peace." After a little more codling, she said she wanted some water, and walked away.

Ruby's was a brilliant admission: she'd been to The Grab Bar where we knew the victim had been.

I called the office, gave them the information, and asked them to get a warrant to search Diane's house. I hope we've got enough, but right now, that's their problem, not mine.

I walked back into Ruby's hospital room. Scotty was still asking about the bar. "Did you have a drink?"

"Yes."

"What kind?"

"A wine spritzer."

Scotty kept badgering her, trying to find out if she had really been there.

"Someone bought my drink for me."

Somebody? This was going to take forever. At least it gave us time to search their homes without their being aware.

Scotty got an email and walked out of the room, leaving Ruby and me alone. I gave her a kind smile. And she talked. Ruby admitted being at The Grab Bar with Clive Benning. It felt so good to hear those words. It took a little work, and getting rid of Diane, but it worked. She was not only there, but there with Benning. Scotty came back in.

"Detective O'Reilly, Ms. Fisher has said she was at The Grab Bar with Mr. Benning last night."

"I remember the music was really loud and it seemed confusing. So when I saw a familiar face, I went over to say 'hi.' I didn't know his name, but I knew his face. Clive has a reputation at work."

Now I wasn't sure if she was parroting back what we said, or giving us valuable new information.

"I don't think any of us are safe with him. Not alone, anyway. I... Cath told me that Brenda fell for him. But he broke her heart."

"Do you know Brenda's last name?" We hadn't come across this name yet.

"Gallagher. Brenda Gallagher. She works the metal sheet fabrication line. Cath said she saw them together, out the back of the building. They were making out."

Scotty walked out, probably to ask the team to find out who Brenda Gallagher was. In the meantime, Ruby was back to minimizing the situation.

She'd gone from being alone to going out alone. From not knowing who Clive was, to being at a bar with him. From saying he was a good guy to being a problem.

"Back to the bar."

"I feel like this is getting overblown."

"When you have nothing to go on, every morsel is important."

"Okay. I didn't go home for dinner. I met Clive before heading to the bar. We had a bite to eat, and then went to The Grab Bar for a drink."

"What's the diner?"

"Mildred's. At the gas station off Highway 23. Yes. I'm sorry I wasn't upfront about Clive. It's...well, I don't want a reputation. Cath can be quite the gossip."

"What would she gossip about?"

"Clive and I were necking. I...I've never kissed a man with a beard. It's like kissing a teddy bear. Not that I know what that's like. It's what I imagine."

"Necking with Clive."

"But he was being weird."

"Weird how?"

"I close my eyes when I kiss someone. But every time I opened my eyes, his eyes were open. And he was not looking at me. He was looking past me."

"At what?"

"He said someone was watching us kiss. I didn't see who."

"Watching you?"

"Yes."

"But you never saw the person."

"No. But Clive was so freaked out, he left. And then I left. I saw him pull out of the parking lot. Then I drove home. Tried to drive home."

"Then you crashed."

She had placed herself at the gas station and the bar with Benning on the night he died. It felt so good to know we were closing in.

CHAPTER 21

"So Clive thought someone at the bar was watching?"

"Yes."

"Like, the bartender? Or wait staff? Or a patron?"

"I don't know, he didn't tell me."

We weren't getting far with her answers, but we sure were pressuring her. Politely, of course. There was something about her that made me want to squeeze the ever-loving truth out of her.

"Did you notice anyone you thought was out of place?"

"No. I don't think I even looked around. I wasn't much interested in what was going on around me."

"Sure, I understand. So you and Clive were kissing, and he got upset?"

"Upset someone was watching us. So he left."

"And when did you leave?"

"A few minutes after. I wa...I wanted to finish my drink."

I could feel my phone buzz in my hand, but didn't want to interrupt the questioning.

"And you had a beer?"

"A wine spritzer."

"And you finished it and left the bar a few minutes after Clive?"

Ruby's frustration was palpable as she threw her hands up in exasperation. "Oh my gosh, how many times do I have to tell you?"

"I'm sorry Ruby. You see, we don't want to be rude. We're listening, to every word. But it's a complex matter. You know how complex this is, I can see it in your face. So we have to hear it a few times to get it through our heads. You see?"

That sounded almost plausible.

We have footage from The Grab Bar and Mildred's. Mildred's is a diner attached to the gas station on Wilmer, before you get on Highway 23. It is a popular place. People could hang out for hours with a coffee, waiting for or selling drugs. No one ever went to Mildred's for food, not ever.

Someone on the team watched video of Ruby and Clive arriving, sitting at a booth. They eat, talk and leave. It took them 58 minutes, and only the server approached them. As Ruby said, the server was in her early twenties, with light hair.

A member of the Homicide squad had already interviewed her, and we had a summary text: 'Waitress confirm Ruby and Clive, nothing special.'

'Did they have hamburgers?'

'Ruby plate fries, Clive hmbuger. *hamburger'

That was close to what Ruby said, I guess.

'How pay?'

'Ruby cash, Clive credit.'

A couple of minor things, since Ruby had said she ate a hamburger. I'll chalk it up to exhaustion. I had to wonder how tired Ruby was, or how much was an act. Every time I thought it was real, that she was on the verge of collapse, she'd perk right up and begin again. I don't think it's tied to Diane's presence. There's something else inside her.

A food service aide arrived and presented Ruby with a covered plate and some milk.

"Can I eat?"

"Yes please. Maybe we should grab a bite in the cafeteria."

"Sure, yeah. We'll be back in a little while. We'll let you eat in peace."

Scotty and I headed out. We'll give her 20 minutes while we get more information.

The hospital was bustling with a steady stream of visitors, perhaps those who had finally finished their work for the day and had time to visit loved ones.

I know the feeling. When Sam is in the hospital, I show up after work. Being a cop, I can get in at all hours. So if I work until 3:00 a.m., I can still visit. If she's asleep, I sit and go through work stuff. If she's awake - and she often is - then we chat.

Scotty and I navigated through the busy halls until we reached the parking lot where Scotty's car sat waiting. The sun was setting in a fiery orange sky, casting long shadows across the pavement and painting everything in warm hues.

Outside, the sound of car horns and distant chatter filled the air, a stark contrast to the quiet and somber atmosphere inside the hospital walls. As we settled into the car to talk, the faint scent of antiseptic lingered on our clothes, a reminder of the sterile environment inside.

The problem with Scotty's car is, it smells like gardenias. A fake, chemical smell pretending to be gardenias, anyway. And the mix with the hospital smell was revolting.

"Dude, why don't you buy a potpourri or something?"

"Right, let me put a container of pine cones and orange peel on my dash board. Maybe some of those spiky brown things."

"Cloves?"

"How should I know? I don't use potpourri, now do I?"

"Snarky much?"

"I'm sick of these two women already. I mean, I can usually interview a suspect for 10, maybe 12 hours. But these two? I've already had enough."

"Okay, let's check what's come in. Give me five minutes while I read over all my messages."

Scotty and I read over all of the text and email messages we'd received. We were so engrossed in our work, I almost missed Diane exiting the hospital. Thankfully, I did notice. She opened the trunk of a blue Amery Falcon, pulled out a hoodie, and closed the trunk. Nothing incriminating, unfortunately. She went back inside, and I headed over to look at the car.

The driver's side had some damage. Clearly she'd been sideswiped. I texted Andrews: 'Tell me about Fisher car damage.'

Within seconds, my phone rang. I really didn't want to talk, I wanted it in writing. I answered anyway.

"We've tracked the paint. It's a factory coat for an Amery Falcon, made in the last five years."

"Can you run a license plate check for me?"

I gave him the tag number of the blue Amery Falcon, and waited a few minutes. The sun was a beautiful golden color, barely starting to go dark.

"The car is registered to Eunice Emerat."

"Thanks. Be sure to note that you told me at...6:24p.m." I headed back to Scotty's car.

"Whatcha doin' Miss Sleuthy-Sleuth?"

'Details on Eunice Emerat? Assoc. w. Diane.'

"I texted the team. The car that Diane got the hoodie from, is registered to Eunice Emerat. So either that's a fake name..."

"Or a relative. Not a big deal."

"What do you think of the idea that Diane killed Clive, maybe out of envy, and then ran Ruby off the road? Diane's car has damage. Well, Eunice's car. And that's why it's a big deal. We will have to ask Eunice about the damage."

My phone buzzed. 'Eunice Emerat, 85. Lives 1414 Fairbrook Lane. Same as Diane.'

'Talk to Eunice about the damage, find out if it's her damage and when it happened.'

"Eunice lives with Diane. So a close relative."

"Okay, so we have a couple of theories. Ruby killed Clive, crashed her car. Ruby killed Clive, Diane found out, forced Ruby off the road. Diane killed Clive, Ruby found out, and ended up off-road. Or Diane killed Clive, Ruby has no idea, and the crash is a coincidence."

"Not a coincidence. The blood and knife tie Ruby to the scene, and the blonde hair ties Diane to the scene."

"So it's like that movie, where the two lesbians team up to kill men at bars?"

"I think there have been a dozen movies like that."

"Do you think either one is in danger from the other?"

"Maybe. We should get back into the room before something bad happens."

We headed back into Ruby's room, arriving in time for Diane to cough all over Ruby. That's a very slow way to kill someone, if that's her intention.

"You should wear a mask if you have something contagious."

"It's something in my throat."

"Same rules as before, Diane. No interruptions."

She looked apologetic. Like a dog that stole the steak right off your plate and let you watch it wolf the thing down.

CHAPTER 22

"Ruby, tell us about your drive home. About the crash."

Ruby looked at Diane, though it was hard to figure out why. She told us there was a near crash by the parking lot, and then she was followed by a dark car. Blue or black.

"What roads did you take?"

"Probably Decker Road to Highway 21, over to 23, then Old Weller Road."

"Probably? Do you remember exactly?"

"Not really. But that's the route I always take–from work. I pass The Grab Bar all the time. You know, one thing I remember..."

Ruby began to reconstruct, or construct, a driving route that made no sense. From The Grab Bar to her home is a short drive, taking Highway 23 to Old Weller to Yurton.

There would be no reason to go onto Highway 21, but she did. It would add at least 10 minutes to your drive.

"You crashed on Old Weller."

"Whereabouts in Old Weller?"

"Six hundred yards east of Yurton. There's a culvert, and a telephone pole. You went into the culvert and hit the pole."

"The pole with the cross on it?"

"How do you know about that pole, Diane?"

"Well, Ruby and I are best friends. I've been to her house. I know the pole."

Feasible, I suppose. Ruby then went on very dramatically about being run off the road. Scott played to her drama, I only asked the sensible questions, of course.

"I was on Old Weller... there were lights. Car headlights."

"Behind you?"

"In front. God! I remember now! The car in front came way over and I had to yank. Yank the steering wheel."

We already knew the damage to her car wasn't fresh, so her theatrics were informative, but a lie. She mimed the crash for us, throwing her hands about and holding her ears because of the loud sounds she's pretending to hear.

We played along as more vehicles became involved. A truck passed, a car followed. It was hard to tell if Ruby was making up the details, or remembering them a little more clearly. And of course, Diane continued to interrupt the conversation. It's like she can't help it.

Ruby is still miming her crash. "There was something. Someone knocked on the window. No! Broke the window. The glass fell on me. I... I heard...an angel? That sounds silly. I don't believe in angels."

"I bet it was an angel. Angels saved you." I wasn't surprised when Diane got in on the action.

"Something wet."

"Wet?"

"I think I wet myself. But it was by my head, so I'm not sure. But then nothing. I could hear nothing. Everything was hazy. Then black."

Ruby started to cry, so I handed her some tissues. In response, Diane put her arm around Ruby.

"What next? After the black?"

"Light. The sun was coming up and I woke up. I thought it was the weirdest dream ever. A man was asking me my name. I don't know what I said."

"You started singing."

"I can't sing. That poor man. Who was he?"

"He found you, and called 911."

We asked her to go over it again, and the story changed a little. This time, the angel laughed.

Ruby was working herself up into hysterics. Diane left the room but returned quickly with a nurse who asked us to leave while she tended to Ruby's sudden panic attack.

"Have you seen the cost of parking?"

"Yep. Crazy expensive. Did you drive, or take the bus?"

"I drove. This is crazy expensive. I might charge the county!" Diane laughed until she saw that neither of us even cracked a smile.

The nurse stepped out of Ruby's room, and we all walked back inside.

"The doctor is on his way."

"We'll leave when he arrives."

"I'd like you to go over it one more time. Please"

Ruby went over the evening again. They arrived separately but at the same time, but Benning was first. The music was loud, they had a drink, maybe two, and started making out. Benning was paranoid, thought someone was watching. Ruby never saw who it was. They left the bar and went their separate ways. Someone followed her, then stopped following her on the highway. Someone ran her off the road and came to her car. A laughing angel. She blacked out. She was rescued. What a load of crap.

Scotty looked at me, and I nodded back. It was time.

"What about the knife?"

The look on her face was priceless. "I..."

"We are going to check your car's GPS."

"I don't have GPS."

"Your car does. Maybe you didn't realize it but–"

"I realized it. I disabled it. Rather, I took it to the shop and they disabled it."

"When?"

"Maybe three years ago?"

"Why?"

"Honestly...I used to be in a relationship with someone who valued their privacy."

"So you disabled the GPS?"

This was the most suspicious thing I'd heard so far. Disabling the GPS because you're dating someone was a new one on me.

Then I realized, she's gotten us off track. "Can we get back to the knife please?"

"But I don't understand. What knife?"

"There was a knife found in your car."

Ruby tried to play it off as a piece of cutlery, a bread knife from work. She asked if we thought she'd stolen it and Scotty took advantage. When Scotty read her Miranda rights to her, both Ruby and Diane recited along with him. Like kids going through the alphabet by memory. I know people know the Miranda Rights, I wasn't aware that people would say them out loud while being read their rights by a cop. These two were odd. And the games continued.

"Was it a butter knife? I guess I might have had a butter knife in my car. But not from work. I'd have bought it. Though I don't know why it would be in my car."

"A hunting knife."

"A hunting knife? Why would I have a hunting knife?"

"Ruby, please stop answering questions with questions. We're trying to figure out why you would have a hunting knife. Asking us what we're asking you, is not helpful."

"I had no hunting knife in my car. I don't own a hunting knife. I have never owned a hunting knife. That's one of those big spiky things, right? No. Don't own one. How's that for a direct answer?"

I smiled. "That was perfect. You don't own and have never owned a hunting knife. But do you know how a hunting knife got into your car?"

"Maybe when I crashed, it was, like, on the road and it flipped up and landed inside my car."

"That's not very plausible."

"Well, I don't know physics very well. Maybe it's plausible. Are my fingerprints on it?"

I looked at Scotty. That was a great opportunity.

"Can we get your fingerprints, to compare to any we find on the knife?"

"You really should have a lawyer, Ruby."

"I haven't done anything, I don't need a lawyer. Should I give them my fingerprints? You're the medicolegal expert. Sure, take my prints."

Scotty stepped out to contact the team and have them send over someone with a portable fingerprint scanner. Ruby turned her fantastical explanation from 'random knife on road flips into my car' to 'angel is a man who looks like Diane.'

"He said something. A word or two. He...smashed the glass and said something and walked away. He didn't help me at all. He was no angel, that's for sure." There was no smashed glass on the scene.

"Maybe he dropped the knife in her car?"

Scotty's return was perfectly times to hear Diane interfere again. He almost lost it when Diane said that. He couldn't believe the absurdity of her suggestion. But he quickly regained his composure and turned back to Ruby.

"Ruby, we need you to be honest with us. It's hard to understand these wild theories of yours. We found the hunting knife in your car, which means it was in your possession at some point. And the fact that it was found in your car raises some serious questions."

Ruby's face went pale, and her eyes darted around the room as if searching for an escape route.

Scotty leaned in closer, his voice low and steady. "Ruby, lying to us will only make things worse for you. The evidence is stacking against you, and it's in your best interest to tell the truth now."

"I swear, I have no idea how that knife ended up in my car!" She looked genuinely terrified.

Our fingerprint tech–the police station is less than a quarter mile away–walked in, interrupting everything. What rotten timing.

CHAPTER 23

We stepped out of the room while the fingerprint technician did his thing. We needed a little time to talk.

"We didn't get the Emerat warrant. Insufficient information."

"Damn. Anything on Eunice Emerat?"

We both scrolled our phones, looking for whatever came in. "Here! Eunice Emerat. Lives at that house, has the car. Widow. No other children. Her and Diane, it looks like."

"I guess that's why Diane can use her car, maybe she doesn't like to drive."

"Okay, I have–"

Diane burst into the hallway. "How dare you?"

"How dare we what?"

"How dare you accuse Ruby of killing someone."

"We haven't said anything like that."

"Don't you play games with me! I know what you cops are like, asking questions and making accusations. What the hell is wrong with you people? Accusing my best friend of murder? Are you out of your damn minds? You think you can waltz in here and point fingers at someone who has been by my side through thick and thin? Who the hell do you think you are?"

"We didn't–"

"I've known Ruby for years, longer than any of you clowns with your badges and your accusations. She's not capable of murder, and I won't stand here and let you destroy her life! You've got no evidence, no damn proof. I won't let you ruin her because you aren't good Detectives! She is innocent, and I will fight tooth and nail to prove it. You think you can bulldoze over people's lives with your accusations? Well, not this time. Not with her! Not with me! You better reevaluate your damn evidence, find the real killer, and leave my friend the hell alone. Accusing her of murder is a disgrace, and I won't let you destroy everything we've built together!"

And then she left. Scotty and I looked at each other.

"Theatrical much?"

I laughed. "What do you think she meant, through thick and thin? Have we done a background check on these two?"

"Yes. Nothing. Not even a parking ticket."

"There's something not right about Diane."

"There's something not right with both of them. Is this because they're in a relationship? Trying to hide it from us?"

"I don't think so. But maybe. I once heard about a couple who were so closeted that when one of them died, the other was thought to be a deranged stranger with no relationship to the deceased. The family, friends, everyone turned her away because there was no proof of a relationship."

"Photos? Email?"

"Nope. Nothing. This was before cameras in phones. They were too closeted."

"Are you sure that isn't that movie, the one with lesbians through time?"

"Pretty sure. This is almost undercover work we're doing."

"No it's not. We've advised them we are homicide Detectives."

"Yeah, but there's something afoot here."

"Afoot? Something afoot? Beware thy shadowed cloak that veils deceit, for in the tapestry of trust, treachery weaveth a darkened thread, staining loyalty with the venom of its whispered betrayal."

"What's that now, Billy Shakespeare?"

"You started it. No one uses 'afoot' anymore."

"I do. I use it with my kids. They are under foot...No, wait, that's not the same thing. Uh..."

"Forget it. If we tip either of them off... Well, it's a little late for that, isn't it? How do you want to play it? How do we keep them both here, and both talking?"

"Should we bring up the blood?"

"Yeah. We know it's male. Maybe find out if Clive was in her car."

"Or any bleeding man."

"Maybe it was the angel. You never know."

I sighed and looked around the hospital corridor. I haven't worked this hard to get a confession in a while. I spotted a priest coming out of a room further down the hall. I bet I am as good at getting a conversation as him.

"Scotty, hey, could this all be some kind of religious thing?"

"Religious? How?"

I shrugged, my gaze sweeping over the intricate designs etched into the walls by nervous people waiting outside rooms while their loved ones died. Why do people feel the need to carve crap into walls? I guess to say, 'I was here.' A way to make sure that other people know they aren't alone.

"I don't know. But something about this case feels…It's like they are worshipping something."

"You're tired. There's nothing like that here."

"Yeah. I guess I am tired. Away from angels, back to facts. Or non-facts. Could Diane have been in the car?"

"Yeah, what do you make of the passenger window being down, but not broken? Ruby insists there was breaking glass."

"It could be honest confusion, and she could be lying. What about the singing angel and talking man and the knife?"

"Oh geez, I have no idea. Let's ask if Ruby needs any mental health medication, that might help us figure it out."

Scotty and I headed toward the nursing station down the hall. I spoke with a harried nurse while Scotty took a whiz.

"Hi, I'm Detective Temple. We're speaking with a patient here, Ruby Fisher, and I'd like to make sure that we aren't interrupting any medication schedules for her. That we aren't delaying any treatment."

"I can't tell you what she's taking, if anything."

"No, of course not. I need to know, if you've set up a routine for her, that we aren't interfering with that routine."

The nurse checked. She mulled over the screen for a bit and said, "There's no schedule. And as a reminder, visitors must be out by eight."

"I'm not sure we're considered visitors, are we? Being police Detectives and all."

"Well, for the sake of other patients, we'd prefer everyone be gone by eight."

"Okay, thank you. I'll take that under advisement." It wasn't much, but I am now confident that Ruby isn't on medication that would be for mental health issues. I wish I could be that confident with Diane.

"Anything?"

"Did you wash your hands?"

"I always wash my hands."

"You never wash your hands."

"I didn't wash my hands."

"Go wash your hands."

Of all places to wash your hands, you'd think it would be a hospital.

"Clean hands, still wet. So, anything?"

"No. She's not on medication as far as I can tell."

"Sounds good, let's head back to the room."

Suddenly, Diane came back into the hallway. "I'd like to stay here with Ruby and be her assistant. Any problems?"

"No ma'am, no problems if you'd like to be here. But like Ruby, I have to read your Miranda rights. If you want to stay."

"Fine."

Scotty played her perfectly. She said it along with him. It was beautiful, but disturbing. It's like she's a child, and has no idea of the deep hole she's digging herself into. People vary in the degree to which they are suggestible, and although the pair of them seemed like they would be suggestible, they always stepped back from the brink.

Diane walked back into the room. I smiled and winked at Scotty, and we walked back inside.

"Okay Ruby, we need to talk about the knife."

"I've said, I don't know anything about a knife. And I gave you my fingerprints. There is no way on God's green earth my fingerprints are on a knife."

"Can I show you a picture of the knife? It's a little dirty, but maybe you'll recognize it." Scotty opened the app on his phone and showed her a photograph of the knife found in her car. Ruby stared at it for a while.

"I've never seen the knife before."

"Diane? Have you ever seen the knife before?"

"Me? No, of course not. Let me see it again? No. I was…I was at a crime scene, last year, where there was a knife. Not like this, a kitchen knife."

"To be clear, you haven't seen this knife?"

"Never in my life."

"Okay, alright. Let's put that aside and talk about the blood."

CHAPTER 24

I had a feeling that the blood in the car was going to result in another round of 'I don't know' and 'angels did it.'

I have no doubt that Ruby or Diane poured the blood on the seat, though I don't know why. Maybe to cover up some other stain. If it was intended to throw us off, all it did was possibly cement a physical connection to the Benning crime. Unless it was another male's blood. That would make this even more complex. Geez, I hope that blood belongs to Benning.

Ruby was still hysterical, so I texted Andrews. 'Anything on cup found on scene?'

He didn't immediately respond, and I turned my attention back to Ruby and Diane.

"Your bruises are from blunt force. The bleeding you did was very minor."

"Very."

Scotty presented a photo of the blood in Ruby's car. Ruby insisted it was her blood despite it being on the passenger seat. As we expected, Diane leaped in.

"Wait, can I take a look? I'm a medicolegal death investigator, after all." Of course we know that is a lie. I am eager to hear her explanation.

"Sure. Take a look."

"This? This blood here? It's on the passenger side seat back."

"Passenger side, that's right."

"But look at the angle. Do you have other photographs? A good investigator would have photos from multiple angles."

Scotty showed her more. "There! See the direction of the blood flow? Someone has poured this blood into the car, while it was on an angle. Was the car on an angle baby?"

Baby?

"We can check the records from rescue services. They'll confirm if the car was passenger side down."

"We'll have to have our own blood spatter expert evaluate the blood flow." That woman was driving us both crazy.

"Why would anyone pour blood in my car?"

Ruby blamed the mystery man from the bar who suddenly seemed very real to her. The mystery man who watched her at the bar, followed her, got in front of her, ran her off the road, and tried to stab her. Her theory was nonsense, and missed one key fact: it had nothing to do with Clive's death. Ruby then suggested someone ran Clive off the road.

"No. That's not how Clive died."

"How'd he die?"

"Exsanguination."

Ruby started shouting. "No. No no no. No way! You think I killed Clive! No no no no no. You're wrong. You think I stabbed Clive, don't you?"

"They aren't saying that. Are you saying that?"

"Ruby, did you kill Clive Benning?"

"No! No no! I liked Clive. He was a nice guy. I know what people said about him, but he was a nice guy to me. I didn't kill anyone. Not Clive, no one. That's horrible."

Diane leaped in, telling us there would be blood on the perpetrator. Then she told us there would be splatter on Ruby's clothes, and asked us if there was blood on Ruby's clothes.

"We can't discuss that directly. Ruby, are those your shoes?"

Scotty reached under the hospital bed. In a clear plastic bag were a pair of clean, white shoes. No blood, at least not to the naked eye. "Size eight?"

"Yes, I wear a size eight."

"Does it matter what her shoe–oh! You have footprints in blood at the crime scene! You can look at the bottom of her shoes. Look at the bottom. Is there blood?"

Scotty turned over the shoes, and there was no blood. "They're very clean. Are they new?"

"No. I mean, maybe a month old. But I keep my shoes clean, you know?"

"Eight."

"Huh?"

"Eight."

Scotty put the shoes back. I watched as he stared at Diane's shoes. They were smaller. He read a text message and looked at me, wide-eyed. My phone dinged. Scotty sat up.

"Your so-called expert should be able to tell you the shoe type."

"We know the shoe type. Brand and size."

"Well then?"

"Well what? You think we should skip over questions and not do our work properly? That's not how we work. We are thorough. Very thorough." Scotty was snappy.

Cue the crying. I looked at Scotty. We were getting nowhere. I gestured toward the door, as we needed to talk.

We read our updates. One of the painters, Diego Garcia, had confessed to robbing the victim. Benning's laptop was found in the van. There appeared to be no blood on the coveralls, but their street clothes had to be checked more thoroughly. They were covered in paint and it was hard to differentiate that from blood on sight.

Sanchez was clean, but Garcia had prior Break & Enter convictions. Neither had any record of violence.

There was no sign of Eunice Emerat.

"I can't imagine Eunice had anything to do with this."

"Agreed. What about Garcia and Sanchez?"

"Yes, it's possible. Every killer has a first victim. Except, how did they set-up Ruby? Get the knife to her?"

"They have a van. Maybe they really did run her off the road."

"Too coincidental."

"Bite to eat?"

"Yeah. I've got to text Sam, let her know I won't be home for dinner."

'Hey gorgeous. Case is taking a while. Can't make dinner.'

Her response was to send me a video of her and the kids making faces and booing noises. I love that woman.

"Is that your kids booing you?"

"Yep. They love doing that."

"If you want to talk to them while you eat, I can leave."

"No. The sooner we nail this case, the sooner I can actually get back to them."

"Well aren't you the sweetest thing."

I stuck my tongue out at him. "Do we have any unaccounted for suspects for Benning?"

"We need to check the painters' alibi. Then they are out. There was no mystery person at the bar, no one proceeded or followed them for five minutes. IT pulled the bar's video and scrubbed through it."

"What about the person the neighbor saw?"

"We don't have enough to–"

I got a text message from Andrews. Ruby Fisher's car received a parking ticket at 12:34 this morning on a street around the corner from Benning's home.

"So, Ruby denied knowing Clive, then we find out she went for dinner and drinks."

"We know Ruby was around Clive's house at 12:34 a.m. Thursday morning, despite saying she went home and not to Clive's after the bar. And the neighbor saw the limping person in Clive's back yard around 1:30 a.m."

"Ruby's car was found at 5:46 a.m. on Old Weller Road. So she crashed sometime between 12:34 a.m. and 5:46

a.m. She had lots of time to commit the murder and stage her incredibly slow car crash."

"And we know the damage to her car is weeks old, so she's lying about being run off the road."

"Yeah, it could have happened without contact. But no, it didn't happen. She drove about 30 feet on the side of the road. That's not a hit and run."

"Had anyone spoken to Peachtree Sales?"

"Uh, no. Not yet."

"Can you arrange that? I want to talk to the doctor, find out if Ruby has a limp. In both legs."

It took a while to track down Dr. Galliano. I found him in the cafeteria, half asleep at a table.

"Doctor, about Ruby Fisher…"

"What now, Detective?" I did not like his attitude.

"Is there any reason Ruby would be limping? Any existing problem with her legs?"

"I'm not sure I can answer that."

"I had reports that she was limping before the accident. I want to find out if she's getting the right treatment. I'll be crucified if work finds out she has a leg problem that isn't being addressed under my care."

"Detective whatever your name is. Ruby is under my care. Not yours. I appreciate that you need to know. I can tell you that no, she had no existing medical condition I am aware of that would cause her to limp. Whoever gave you that information is incorrect. Now, if you don't mind, leave me alone. For a few minutes at least, hmm?"

What a snotty guy. That Ruby doesn't have a limp, or at least no reason to limp, isn't helpful.

It seems like every time we find something to suspect her, we find something else to exonerate her. Now, Diane is a whole other issue.

CHAPTER 25

"Clive Benning was found dead this morning in his home. A couple of painters had arrived to do some work, and found him. Early estimate is, he died sometime late last night or the early morning. From stab wounds from a large knife with a serrated edge. The wounds generally match the hunting knife found in your car. Your car, Ruby."

Cue the overacting. "No no no! I didn't kill Clive! I swear! Oh my God. Diane, make it stop, please!"

"Who are the painters? Maybe they killed him."

"And planted the knife?"

"You have to consider it."

"Ruby, do you know these men?" Scotty showed Ruby a photograph of Sanchez and another of Garcia. She didn't know them. As soon as we said they were the ones who found Benning, Diane snapped at the bait.

"So they could have killed Clive. It's not unheard of for the 911 caller to be the killer."

"There was no blood on their coveralls."

"They could have changed. Did you check their van?"

"Of course we did! We're Detectives." Now Diane was ticking me off.

She insisted it was the painters, and when I asked why they would kill him, it was a robbery gone wrong. She wasn't that far-fetched. She suggested they broke in–once she found out they had a key she said they would simply have walked in–and kill him when he discovered them in the home.

"Use the key when he's away. Rob him, but he comes home. Stab him. Then plant the knife on Ruby."

"How would they have known about Ruby?"

"Oh! The person watching Clive and me at the bar?" Had these two discussed this when we were out of the room?

"Yes! One painter watching Clive and...watching you? Anyway, one painter watching and one painter robbing. Then they kill Clive, follow Ruby, run her off the road and frame her."

It was nonsense. They suggested one painter went to the house to kill Clive, the other stayed at the bar to follow Ruby. Diane's theory of painters killing him when he found the men in his home, is out the window. Now she was suggesting they were lying in wait at two scenes: the house and the bar. I figured if we kept them talking, they might reveal bits and pieces of what really happened. By their theory, Clive would have been killed, then the painter had to bring the knife to where Ruby was, to plant it.

Maybe, there were two scenes: Diane at the house to kill Clive, and Ruby to crash her own car to...Nope, there'd be no reason for Ruby to crash her car.

"How did bar painter get the knife ahead of the crime?" It was hilarious that Ruby asked the question we'd have asked. Even she could see the hole in the theory.

"Ruby, how tall are you?" We wanted to compare her height to that of the estimate from the witness near the Benning home.

"Five foot eight. One hundred and thirty pounds, give or take."

"I'm five foot four."

"Blue! The car that charged me was blue. Not black. It was blue. I remember that more." Ruby was changing the conversation again, lying again. I looked at Scotty and he nodded. We'd let her run with it.

"Blue car. Okay, think about the blue car."

"I saw the lights and I screamed and I turned the wheel. There was a loud scraping noise. I guess that's when I hit the pole."

"Scraping sound?"

"Yes. I think I scraped the car. I think he got so close I actually scraped against the car."

"You scraped the car that night? In the accident?"

"Yes. When else would I have done it? My car was fine that morning."

Another lie dug her hole a little deeper. Ruby insisted the damage was done that night, when our own traffic accident expert told us it was at least a week old, maybe older. And Diane again told us how to work. I was a little frustrated. We were off track. These two are surprisingly persuasive.

"Let's park that and get back to Clive."

With some hesitation, Ruby again said she knew Clive. Clearly, she did not want to keep saying that in front of Diane.

"One of my colleagues has had a chance to speak with Steven Cartwright. Do you know Steven?"

"No, who is he?"

"Clive's best friend. He knows who you are."

Ruby went ashen. "I've never heard of Steven."

"Clive texted Steven. The message said...'Ruby from work. She's sad. LOL. Peach. Eggplant. Waterdrops.'" It was a code for sex.

Suddenly, Ruby remembered something about Clive sending a text message that night. Miraculous.

"Clive was a player. And he had a type. He liked to find women who were sad or upset, and be sympathetic. He'd give her a shoulder to cry on, then take her home."

"I didn't go home with him. I left the bar and went home and crashed."

"There's evidence of someone being there with him. At the house. In his bedroom."

I didn't think Ruby could get any paler. And Diane was starting to turn red. "It wasn't me."

It may not have been her. It could have been Diane. Or any of a million other women, apparently. But the hairs, the long blonde hairs. I looked at Diane's hair again. Where is that darn DNA?

"Okay stop asking those questions. Ruby isn't that type of woman."

"What type of woman are you, Ruby? Who's your type?"

"Okay, can I have Ruby alone please?" Dr. Galliano asked us to leave.

We headed out into the hallway. "Diane, you're her best friend. Do you know what her type is?"

"I don't. I thought I did, but clearly I was wrong."

"What did you think it was?"

"It doesn't matter."

The doctor stepped out of the room. Diane went in, but he suggested he wanted to speak to us for a moment.

"Detectives, I expect to release Ruby tomorrow. You'll be able to interrogate her about whatever this is, in your own damn back yard." He stormed away.

"What was that all about?"

"I'm not sure. The medical staff here certainly like Ruby more than us."

Scotty's phone buzzed. "No one at Peachtree had any idea Ruby and Clive were dating."

"Yeah, I honestly don't think they were. Did anyone check with Brenda Gallagher?"

"Who?"

"His ex."

"Unless we have more than a name, I doubt anyone could find her."

"What about–"

Two women walked slowly past us. One with a walker, the other helping her stay steady. In fact, there were a lot of people around. It was a hospital, after all.

"Maybe we should take this outside. Too many ears."

We nodded in agreement and made our way through the bustling hospital corridors. The air was heavy with the scent of antiseptic and the murmur of hushed conversations floated around us. The occasional scream punctuated the quiet. As we walked, I couldn't help but glance into the rooms we passed, catching glimpses of the human drama unfolding.

In one room, a young couple held each other tightly, tears streaming down their faces as they received devastating news. In another, an old woman yelled "Help me! They're killing me!" over and over and over. They weren't really, at least, I doubted it. A nurse was trying to soothe her. It wasn't working.

The hospital was a microcosm of hope and despair, where euphoria and heartbreak coexisted in equal measure.

We finally found an empty corridor away from prying eyes and leaned against the wall. Scotty checked his phone for any updates while I stared absentmindedly at a beige painting on the wall, its faded colors reminiscent of better days. Why would anyone buy a beige painting?

CHAPTER 26

Outside the hospital, Scotty and I started making phone calls. I called the office to find out if they had given any insight into denying the Emerat warrant. He'd simply said there was insufficient information.

I called the Forensic office. They had a few pieces of information for me. They used a rapid DNA system to confirm that the DNA in the blood in the cup found near the scene, on the knife and on the car seat were the same as Clive Benning's. While more thorough tests would be run later, it gave us valuable information now. It absolutely tied Ruby to Clive's death.

They had a preliminary DNA profile of the blonde hair found at the scene, and it matched that found on the woman's top. The top also has Clive's blood on it. We hadn't matched that to anyone, but Diane has long blonde hair. We didn't have her DNA yet.

Ruby's footwear was clean, and the wrong size to match the prints find at Clive's house. And although Diane's footwear was also clean, and the wrong brand, it was the right size.

A different woman's DNA was located in the bedroom.

If we could get Diane's DNA, we could probably get our warrant. But it was unlikely to happen.

Scotty called the office back and asked them to try to get a court order for DNA for Ruby and Diane.

"You should know, I've used the Bachmeyer Maneuver." Scotty loved that trick. He carried an empty, unused phone with him. He would use Near-field Communications to place some information on the phone, then leave it available to a suspect to see what happens. It was legal, but a little underhanded.

"I want to speak to Ruby's family members. Do we have their contact information?"

"I do. Her mother, lives in Florida."

I called Patty-Lou Fisher.

"Hello, my name is Francine Temple. I'm with the Little Bluff Police. I'd like to–"

"Now what did she do?"

"If this Patty-Lou Fisher?"

"Yes. And my daughter is Ruby Fisher. What'd she do?"

"She was in a minor car accident. She's okay. She's at–"

"Don't care, don't tell me."

I was shocked by her responses. I decided I might as well grab the bull by the horns.

"Can you tell me what's between you?"

"Being Ruby's mom, I can tell you it was a messed-up relationship between her and Diane out there in Little Bluffs. I don't mean one of those kinds of relationships. You know. I mean, Ruby was always sickly, and prone to daydreaming. Poor girl didn't have a lot of friends growing up because she was always sick. But then along comes that Diane, who basically fused right into Ruby's little fantasy world. It was unnatural. They wrote stories and even created their own, I don't know, faith I guess."

"How long have they known each other?"

"Since fifth grade. Diane was the weirdest best friend a girl could ever have. Diane has a whole lot of anger going on, and she could really stir up some strange vibes with Ruby."

Since fifth grade? I hadn't seen that one coming. "So you didn't like Diane?"

"That part isn't really what matters. I can tell you, they were hooked on each other in a way that didn't leave room for good sense or common decency. Diane turned Ruby's world upside down. Diane wrecks everything in her path."

"Was there a specific event?"

"No. Watching my once lively daughter get tangled up in Diane's drama was like seeing a train wreck in slow motion. Their friendship was this crazy ride that left scars on everything around. I told her to never call me until she stops being friends with that woman. I'm sure Diane's mother will tell you the same thing."

"Have you spoken to Eunice recently?"

"Oh, not for a good year."

"Okay, thank you. If you'd like to get in touch with your daughter–" I looked at the phone. She'd hung up.

"Have we located Eunice Emerat yet?"

"Nope."

I told Scotty what Patty-Lou had told me.

"Didn't they both say they've known each other for a few years?"

"I thought so. But with these two, it's hard to tell what's up and what's down sometimes."

We headed back in. Ruby and Diane were talking in the hospital room. We waited outside the door. Listening.

"The Detectives think I killed Clive. That I stabbed him and drove off with the knife. They think I killed a man."

"You're right baby, I think they think that. But I don't think that. I know you better than they do."

"But that knife." Scotty left to get coffee at the nearby vending machine while I continued to listen.

"Look, I've been thinking. This could all be a set-up." Diane concocted another theory where a killer set up Ruby to take the fall. She knew about the shortcut be-tween Clive's home and Ruby's crash scene. She then sug-gested that the killer forced Ruby off the road specifically to plant evidence. But the killer was smart enough to not put Ruby's prints in the dried blood on the knife.

Then Diane floored me by suggesting we would find a cup with blood in it near the crash scene. When Scotty returned with the coffee, I updated him. He peaked into the room.

"She has the phone in her hands. Diane's got the phone."

We gave them a few more minutes to keep looking at the information Scotty had selected. We walked in and Scotty snatched the phone out of her hands.

"You're interfering with the investigation."

"I have a theory."

"I don't care."

"No, let's hear her out." Good cop, bad cop.

"Clive has an affair with a married woman. Her husband finds out, and tracks him down to the bar. He's the mystery man Clive saw at the bar. Clive leaves, hubby follows him to his house. Hubby confronts Clive, they tussle, Clive is stabbed. Hubby flees with the knife and a sample of blood in order to set someone up. He takes a shortcut to Old Weller Road, and chooses the first car he sees. Ruby's. He runs her off the road, leaves the knife and some blood on the car. And he's away."

"That's quite a theory. You're missing some key points, though."

"Like what?"

"Like the damage to the car. Your problem is, you don't have all the information. All the evidence. So you concoct these crazy theories based on nothing."

"That's harsh."

"What about the painters?"

I gave them a big smile. "They've been arrested for theft from Clive Benning's house."

There was an immediate leap from thieves to murderers. Diane dropped her enraged husband theory and suggested it was the painters who were the killers.

"Look, Ruby. We'd like to speak to you tomorrow. Maybe at the police station?"

"I guess so. If they release me."

"I'll leave my card. Give me a call." I left my card on the table beside the hospital bed, and we headed out.

"What do you think?"

"I think they are in it together. We need that warrant on Diane's house, and for their DNA."

Scotty and I each headed home.

"Hey babe! I'm home!" I walked in to a bunch of happy faces watching television. The kids waved and Sam pointed to a glass of wine she'd poured for me. I ran upstairs, changed, grabbed my laptop, and headed back downstairs.

"Have you eaten? Leftovers in the fridge."

I dropped my laptop on my chair, grabbed my dinner from the fridge, and bent over Sam to kiss her.

"Thanks babe."

"Long day not over yet?"

"Nah. You know me. I want to read over all the reports. Thanks for the wine. New scarf?"

Sam touched her head. "Yes, you like it?"

"Roses, very classy. Didi, do you–"

"Right here!" Didi pulled out an identical scarf. Any time Sam bought a new one, Didi wanted the same scarf. She'd wear it over her head, like her mom Except, of course, Sam's head was bald while Didi's was full of curly locks.

"Can you play Dash'N'Dodge with me tonight?"

"Of course." I love the game so much, I sometimes don't let Tony win. I'd let him win tonight. I had other things on my mind.

CHAPTER 27

D r. Galliano called me this morning. He'd seen my business card on Ruby's table. He asked for Scotty and I to come to the hospital, Ruby may have attempted suicide.

"What do you mean, 'may have'?"

"We don't know for certain how she was exposed, but it appears she has ingested sodium hypochlorite. It's in a cleaning agent."

"Cleaning agent, as in...?"

"A disinfectant and bleaching agent."

"Bleach? She ingested bleach?"

"Yes." Now he could have said she drank bleach, that would be easier, wouldn't it?

"On my way."

The problem with being a Detective is, you're always available. Even if you're asleep, you carry your office phone with you. I call Scotty, and asked that we meet at the hospital. He suggests a coffee shop around the corner.

I kiss Sam goodbye, she's always so good about these things, and I head out. The morning sun hasn't risen, but the air is crisp and clear.

Little Bluff has a beautiful downtown. The outskirts, like so many other places, are a lot rougher. I don't mean the land, I mean the people. They seem to either be terrified or angry. I suppose some people are terrified by the angry people, and some people are angry that people are terrified. There is a high level of drug use, assaults, drunk driving and robbery. I mean, we're big enough to have a Homicide Division.

But we keep our downtown pretty and quaint. It fools the tourists and keeps the dollars flowing. You can buy handmade pottery that sits a little crooked and candy made by people who don't wear gloves or wash their hands properly. There are antique shops full of barn discards and, of course, coffee shops.

Scotty and I meet at The Silver Badge, a place popular with cops.

"Before anything, I should tell you, I looked over the files and resubmitted a search warrant request for Diane's home. I'm hoping it gets signed today."

"We didn't get any new information."

"I know, but I wrote it instead of Lambton. I can be a little more linear in my logic than him. Helps with the understanding."

"I hope so. So what do you think? A suicide attempt?"

"I doubt it. That's an ineffective and painful way to go. Now, it could be that Diane gave her a little something after we'd gone."

"What would she have to gain by that?"

"In case you hadn't noticed, those two have a pretty strange relationship. I'd say Diane is controlling, maybe even abusive. You've notice the way Ruby starts sometimes. And Ruby's mother mentioned illnesses and a fantasy world."

"Yeah, something's up. Ruby acts like she's afraid of getting hit. I guess it's possible Diane poisoned her to, what? Teach her a lesson?"

"Yes. There are no domestic incident reports, but remember she talked about being in a relationship with a private person? Disabling her GPS and stuff? Maybe she was forced to."

"Maybe. You'd think if Diane was controlling, the tracking would be active and she'd be monitored."

"Huh. You're right. Damn, we need a warrant for Ruby's phone. I'll call the office, leave a message for Taylor. You clean the table like a good boy."

I left a message asking Detective Taylor to obtain a warrant for her phone. Overnight, I'd read the reports from the analysts at Ruby's house. They found nothing of apparent value to us. Nothing. There are fingerprints that are not hers. They confiscated a baggie labeled 'catnip' because Ruby does not appear to have a cat. There was a laptop computer, which is yet to be analyzed. No traces of blood, no weaponry, no telling magazines. Nothing.

Scotty and I left and met up again at the hospital. We went first to Dr. Galliano.

"Detectives, it would appear that last night, Ruby Fisher ingested sodium hypochlorite. Bleach. As I said. That's based on the nurse finding the bottle near the bed. Not a large amount, but enough to make her ill. Her mouth and esophagus show signs of damage, but I expect that to heal without issue."

"Is the bottle of bleach still by her bedside?"

"No. It was removed, in case she had voluntarily ingested it and wanted to try again. We've moved her to another room, closer to the nursing station."

"We need that bottle."

"Talk to the nurse."

He was very curt. We followed him into Ruby's room. Upon seeing us, she cried.

"Hi Ruby. How are you feeling?"

"Okay I guess."

"Did you know what happened last night?"

"No?"

"What do you remember?"

"You left. Diane left. I fell asleep. The nurse woke me up and said I'd had a seizure."

"Did you eat or drink anything?"

"No."

"The doctor is concerned you might have tried to hurt yourself."

"I think the world is already handling that quite well, thank you."

"You didn't try to hurt yourself?"

"No. I didn't try to hurt myself. I didn't–"

Diane walked in with a coffee.

"I didn't hurt Clive. I didn't hurt anyone."

Scotty headed out to find the bleach. I shut the door for a little more privacy.

"We had a chance to talk more with the painters. They did rob Clive's house. We have them for that. But they have solid alibis for the evening when Clive died."

Ruby's heart monitor showed her pulse increasing. "We have a statement from Cliff's neighbor, a guy who was getting home from work at 10:45 p.m. He saw someone leave Clive's house. A woman. Ruby. They described a person about five foot five, and about one hundred and thirty pounds. Sound familiar?"

Scotty came back in and whispered in my ear. "Got the bleach and garbage. Bleach in a coffee cup."

"Ruby?"

"Clive and I were dating. I didn't see him after we went to the bar. Not that night. But we were dating."

Diane slammed the foot bar of the hospital bed and stormed out. She was furious. Maybe the theory of Diane poisoning Ruby wasn't that far-fetched after all.

Ruby admitted to being at Clive's on multiple occasions. This would be a good reason to get her DNA if the search warrant failed. She denied being there on Wednesday evening, but said she'd been there multiple times.

"You check with your eye witness. You'll find out the date is wrong. I'd been over a few times. You'll find my DNA somewhere I'm sure. But he had a thing about cleaning, so I have no idea how much."

"A thing about cleaning?"

"Yes. God, yes. He'd clean everything. That guy would wash the dishes right after using them. Clive would even vacuum while I was still there. He scrubbed the toilet bowl after a...number two."

I've been in that house. He absolutely did not clean his toilet. Ever, I imagined.

I tuned back into Ruby's denials. She was talking about Clive having a dispute with a neighbor. "He told me they almost came to blows about it."

"Why are you mentioning this now? Why not earlier when I asked if you knew anyone Clive was feuding with?"

She said there wasn't, and resented being questioned. "I should be at home with a nice glass of wine and a little music on, reading a good book. Even a terrible book. But I certainly shouldn't be lying in a hospital bed talking to Detectives about my boyfriend's murder."

The look on Diane's face when Ruby said 'boyfriend'! I can clearly see the possibility of poison.

"Did you have sex?"

"Not full-on sex, no. But we fooled around."

"Necking?"

"Yes."

"Who else knew about the two of you?"

"No one. No one that I know of, anyway. I don't know what Clive told anyone. You'd have to ask around."

A nurse popped in to take Ruby's vitals, so we all left the room. Scotty had already contacted the Forensic Unit about the bleach and garbage, so it wasn't long before a tech texted to say he was outside and waiting. Scotty took it out to him.

One thing was for sure, Ruby was not going to be interviewed at the station today.

CHAPTER 28

The nurse left, and Diane went into the room. I waited for Scotty to return, listening at the door.

"Who the hell do you think you are? You never told me about this. I mean, what the hell, Ruby? Clive? Are you serious?"

"Diane, hear me out–"

"No! I don't want to hear a damn thing. You lied to me even worse than before. You were with him while I wanted to fix things."

"I didn't know you wanted to fix anything. You were sleeping with your secretary for God's sake!"

Luscious gossip to be sure. Scotty came back, and we both listened.

"Were you going to live together or something? I guess not now. Not if he's dead. I can't believe I wanted you back. I can't believe I wanted us back! You dated him and he died. Horribly. Maybe there's a lesson to be learned."

"A lesson to be learned? What does that mean? Why are you being so mean to me?"

"You can turn off the fake tears, you two-timer! I know they're fake." This was great. I held my breath, hoping that there would be an accusation, maybe some real tears. But it came to nothing.

We had to intervene. "Is everything okay in here? Diane, you seem to be taking Ruby's relationship with Clive quite personally."

"I am not."

"Yes, you are."

"Look, Ruby is a little...naïve. I said it before. She doesn't know what she gets herself into sometimes."

"What's it to you though?"

"We're best friends."

"Is there more to your relationship?"

"Of course not."

Ruby lost it. "You've always been such a good liar. Yes! Yes Diane and I were in a relationship. She broke it off to be with her secretary, and now she wants back with me. I should have listened to your mother and left you a long time ago."

From the way Diane steamed up so quickly, it was clearly a sore spot. We really needed to talk to Eunice Emerat.

"You take that back. She doesn't know what she's saying. She's on medication, she's saying things."

"If one of you will get me my phone, I can prove it."

We wouldn't even need a warrant! I picked up Ruby's phone from the bedside table–unnecessary since it was in her reach, but it felt like the dramatic thing to do. I gave her the phone and she unlocked it, opened up the photo app, and handed it back. There were photos of them together. Nothing romantic, but lots of photos together.

They kept yelling at each other. Diane is so deeply in the closet, she can't bear the thought of being outed. While I was busy with the phone, Diane lunged for Ruby. Scotty reached out to stop her, and she shrank back immediately. Now, that was a woman who really hated men.

It was possible that this hatred translated into murder. Although, given the wounds, she'd have had to get very close. Maybe hold him. Not tight, mind you, I don't think she'd have been able to hold him down. She's too slight for that. But a hug isn't a hold. Maybe she hugged him.

Now that was settled, I went back to the photos on her phone. Them in front of a building. Them in a backyard sitting. Duck face, duck face, tongue sticking out selfie.

I looked through a few more photos before I found it. "Scott?" He came over the looked.

I whispered. "A photograph of Diane in a shirt that looked a lot like what we'd found at the scene."

"Diane, can I speak to you outside?" Scotty and Diane left the room. I stayed with Ruby and asked her about her relationship with Diane.

They'd been in a relationship for about three years. As she spoke, Ruby made excuses for Diane's bullying and secretive behavior.

"You know, I used to think it was kind of romantic. All this secrecy and intensity. I mean, almost like we were sneaking around. In fact, we were sneaking around. If word got out that she likes women, she'd probably lose her investigator position. Although, dating the secretary is probably not too discreet, hmm?"

Why on earth would she think Diane would lose her position for coming out? Then again, that wasn't actually her title. At least Ruby had been honest with us.

"Did she ever hit you? Or hurt you?"

"Not really. Nothing I went to see a doctor about."

That qualifier caught my attention. Nothing to see a doctor about.

"Did she ever threaten you? Threaten to hurt you for any reason?"

"Diane is complicated. She likes to be the center of attention, she likes to be in control. You've noticed that, I'm sure."

I pressed a little more, asked if she ever got the authorities involved.

"She came over to my house, pretty angry, and we got into a fight. It got, I don't know, a little scary I guess. I called police. They showed up but by then, Diane was back to her old self. Very sophisticated, you know? You've seen how she can be. She told the police it was mostly my fault, that I called them to get her into trouble. I didn't...I didn't really say anything. I mean, what could I say? She was being mean to me? That's childish. So I didn't say much of anything. And the police officers kind of got angry for wasting their time and they left. I didn't get their names or anything. Police officers in uniform."

"Did they make a report?" They'd have made a report, to explain their time spent at a call if nothing else.

"If they did, they didn't tell me about it. No one called back or anything like that."

Ruby said Diane would say the incident never happened. I wasn't sure. There should have been a report, but sometimes, with the wrong cops, they don't bother.

"Honestly, I was pretty devastated. It had been three years before she dumped me. I guess I was...lonely. I guess that's where Clive comes into the picture. Like you said, he can lend a sympathetic ear."

"But you didn't sleep together?"

"No. I wasn't ready for that yet."

"And you were together on the night he died? And you were sad and lonely, but you ended up going home alone?"

"Yes, because Clive was getting paranoid."

"About someone following him. And then you left."

"And someone followed me, but then went away."

"And then someone drove you off the road and came over to you, but didn't help. Right?"

"That's right. The person didn't help me."

I leaned back in my chair and stared at her phone. There were photographs. Of course there were other apps. There was email and social media apps. They might track her if she had location services on. The phone service was active, so cell towers would be able to locate her. I wondered if she had actually been as anonymous as she thought.

My phone buzzed. Yes! The team was executing the search warrant on Diane's house. I was hoping we might find evidence of her purchasing a hunting knife, or using her computer to search 'how to frame your ex.' I'd take anything at this point.

I wanted to open up all of the apps on Ruby's phone, find out what she'd been up to. But I only dared look at the photos. I wanted no activity to be registered on the phone that could be called into question by a defense attorney.

I went out to get Scotty and Diane. She was sullenly sitting with her back to the wall, arms crossed. Scotty was beside her, ignoring her, going through his phone. I hope he has something for us.

Chapter 29

Scotty and I nodded to each other in silent agreement. It was time to confront Diane about the shirt.

We all walked into Ruby's hospital room. I showed Diane the photograph of her and Ruby, the one where she is wearing the blue shirt.

"Diane, can you explain this photograph to us?"

She said she and Ruby had gone to Aruba on vacation, as friends, of course.

"That's a lovely photograph of the two of you smiling. That...that's a nice top. Did you buy it there?"

"Umm, yes, the blue number. It is beautiful, very affordable there."

"Do you two ever swap tops?"

"We're quite different sizes. In case you hadn't noticed, Detective." Ruby was a bit sharp with her tone.

"So no clothing swaps? Between partners?"

Diane froze.

"Why are you lying to us?" I told her Ruby said they'd been in a relationship for three years.

"Lying? I'm not lying. We were together for three years. But you don't know what it's like around here. I could lose my position, lose my pension. Please, don't tell anyone."

"You can't lose anything, Diane, that's against the law. And actually, I do know what it's like. I'm gay, but I'm out and no one cares." Good old Scotty.

"No, not for me. For me, it's different. I get that maybe you don't have to be discreet, but I do."

"There's discreet, and there's secretive."

"So what? So what if I was secretive? It's my secret to keep."

"Hers too. It's Ruby's secret too, to live like that."

"So what? Who cares? We broke up and now...We broke up and Ruby started to date a guy and if you ask me, she killed him. There! I said it! I'm not protecting you anymore. I know exactly how it happened. And if you Detectives haven't figured it out yet, shame on you."

My phone buzzed, but I ignored it.

"I'm the medicolegal death investigator here. I'm the crime scene expert. I saw those photos, I heard the stories. I've been here from the start, I heard everything. Ruby met Clive at a bar, went to his home and for whatever reasons, killed him. Then she took the knife and some blood–maybe to drink later, I don't know."

I looked at Scotty. I didn't understand why Diane was still lying so much. Maybe the two of them really did live in a fantasy world and now that they'd broken up, they had to deal with reality.

My phone buzzed again. I ignored it again.

"She got careless and crashed her car on the way home. I bet there was no other car. There was no person to set you up with a knife. What a ridiculous story. The pour pattern is from where your cup of blood splashed. Ruby, you're sick, you're a sick woman."

My phone buzzed. I finally checked my messages. One of the coffee cups had traces of bleach in it. We had to find out about the bleach. Ruby said she did not drink coffee yesterday, but pointed out that Diane had two cups at one time.

Scotty started filming with his phone.

"Diane, did you have two coffees yesterday? All to yourself?"

"Yes, I suppose so. What of it? Is it a crime now not to give a treacherous woman a coffee?"

"Ruby, did you drink her coffee?"

"I don't understand. She gave me a sip, but I didn't like it."

"I did not!"

"You did too. A sip though, it was too bitter. I've never been one for coffee."

The pair of them fed off each other. Their energies were constantly shifting, but every time one was up, the other was down. They seemed to delight in being contrarian.

My phone buzzed again, and I ignored it.

"Diane, did you know about Clive?"

"What? Of course not."

"Where were you Wednesday night?"

My phone buzzed, and so did Scotty's. While Diane was continuing her denials, we looked at the message that came through. DNA on the coffee cup matched the DNA from the long blonde hair at the Benning scene.

I texted a request for uniformed officers to attend the hospital. I texted the team to prepare for the arrest of Diane Emerat. We finally had enough evidence.

Diane finally refused to answer our questions, and Scotty threatened to arrest her. When she finally did answer, she denied everything. She denied giving Ruby the coffee. She denied the earlier incidence of domestic assault.

Scotty again suggested Diane might be arrested, and she freaked out. She claimed she'd lose her position if she was arrested. Which is also not true.

My phone buzzed.

"Diane Emerat, you have th–"

"No! No way!"

Diane leaped to her feet and tried to run out of the room. We let her run to the door. As soon as she opened it, she saw three uniformed officers. Diane stopped and sat back down.

"Diane Emerat. You have the right to remain silent. Anything you say can and will be used against you in a court of law. You have the right to an attorney. If you cannot afford an attorney, one will be appointed for you. Do you understand these rights?"

"Diane?"

My phone buzzed.

"Yes I understand my rights. But you have no evidence. None! I didn't do it! I didn't kill Clive."

We didn't tell her what we were arresting her for, all we did was read her the Miranda Rights again. It put her in a very panicky frame of mind. I told her the paint transfer on Ruby's car matched a blue Amery Falcon.

Ruby began to scream, setting off the heart monitor. A nurse rushed in but left quickly.

My phone buzzed.

"And we think she tried to kill you, too."

"I fucking did not! You fucking twits! I haven't done anything. She isn't even worth trying to kill!"

My phone buzzed. I finally looked at the damned messages.

'Emerat house. Human body found in basement freezer.'

I almost dropped my phone. I looked at Scotty and motioned for him to read his messages. When he did, he smirked.

Diane suddenly leaped up and tried to attack Ruby. Scotty and I grabbed her and I shouted for the uniformed officers. They quickly got her under control, cuffed her, and stepped out into the hall. "Bring her down to the cruiser."

We had a few more words for Ruby, let her know she might have to testify, and we left.

We followed as they dragged Diane screaming and bucking outside, and to the nearest cruiser. She kicked out her legs, stopping the officers from easily placing her in the back seat. A little like how a cat spreads out and refuses to get into its carrier. The only difference was, Diane didn't bite.

It took all three officers to get her in and buckled up. That was going to be a fun ride to the station.

Everything was up in the air now. A body in a freezer. I did not see that coming at all. We had some great evidence against Diane for the murder of Benning, and probably even enough to charge her with trying to poison Ruby. Did Ruby know about the body in the freezer? Is that ultimately why Diane tried to poison Ruby? Who the hell was it in the freezer, anyway?

"What do you think, partner? Lesbian serial killer?"

"I'm not sure. Do two bodies make a serial killer?"

"I think they should. So, is the body in the freezer Eunice, an ex of Diane's, or some other suitor of Ruby's who mysteriously disappeared?"

"My money's on mom."

"Bet! Ten bucks says it's anyone else but mom. Take it?"

"Yes. You have yourself a bet."

CHAPTER 30

Scotty and I went to the office while uniformed offi-cers took Diane. They put her in an interview room, handcuffing her to the table. She was not happy.

"Do you want something to eat or drink?"

"I didn't fucking kill Clive!"

"Okay, but before we talk about that, do you want something to eat or drink? You're going to be here for a while."

I think that's when it sunk in that she'd be better off helping us than fighting us. She wanted a soda and a sand-wich, which Scotty got for her.

I called the medical examiner.

"The body in the freezer appears human."

"Appears?"

"We can't get at it. Not yet. It seems the body was placed at the bottom of the freezer, and then layers of water were poured on. When the first layer froze, another layer was added. It is a solid block of ice the size of a freezer: 60 by 34 by 26. Underneath that, we think we see a body."

"How long until you know? Until you can get a cause of death?"

"Days. We have to unfreeze it carefully. We can chip away at some of the higher levels of ice, run the remnants through a sieve to catch any evidence. But this will take some time."

"Any idea how long she's been there?"

"None. The freezer is about five years old, if that helps."

Scotty came back and I told him what the examiner had told me. We started pouring over the files.

"Eunice?"

"That's what I'm thinking. Do we have any evidence she's alive?"

"There is some mail addressed to her. A social security letter, a water bill. Geez, did the old woman die and Diane kept cashing the Social Security checks?"

"Wouldn't be the first time that happened."

"Alright, well, we won't charge her with Eunice's murder until we know it's Eunice, and how she died. But there is abuse of a corpse, at least."

"I hope we don't have a serial killer on our hands."

"I doubt it. We only found the one body at the house. Didn't we?"

"Yes, one. Alright, let's focus on Clive Benning. Point, counter-point."

Scotty loved to argue, and he took point.

"Point: DNA from the long blonde hair places the same person at the Benning crime scene. I believe…yes. The long blonde hair from the hairbrush in Ruby's purse matches the hair at the crime scene. It isn't Ruby's, so it must be Diane's."

"Counter-point: We haven't confirmed it's Diane's, but I'll let that pass. You know, that the hair was in Ruby's hairbrush meant she could have taken a few strands and planted it."

"Point: Bloody wet wipe in Ruby's bag has male DNA on it."

"When did you get that information?"

"About 20 minutes ago. Keep up."

"Fink. Counter-point: Uh, maybe blood splashed into the purse when it was poured. I'd say that if I was a defense lawyer. We need to have the whole purse checked."

"Point: Diane has no verifiable alibi for the timeframe Benning was murdered."

"Counter-point: It's suspicious behavior, but not evidence. And neither does Ruby."

"Point: Diane has purposefully turned off all tracking on her car and phone. Do we have her cell records yet?"

"No. So counter-point: It's suspicious behavior, but not evidence. And same for Ruby."

"Point: size six shoe prints at the crime scene. Ruby is eight."

"Ah, that's an interesting one. Counter-point: the neighbor saw someone who limped with both legs. I think that's how she put it. So what if it was Ruby, shoving her size eights into size six shoes, and hobbling as a result. She knows Diane's size."

"True. We could really use a pair of bloody shoes and a bunch of bloody clothing right now. Point, um, point toward a set-up of Diane by Ruby: Ruby claims the car ran her off the road, but the damage is old. The paint comes back to an Amery Falcon, and Diane told us earlier that someone had damaged her car days ago."

"So maybe Ruby hit Diane's car then days later, pulls safely off the side of the road, lightly hits a pole, and claims someone forced her off the road?"

"Well, the idea that a killer would follow then not follow her then run her off the road after killing Benning is far-fetched. Plus, the timelines don't work. Killing and setting up a crime scene takes time."

"And imagination. Ruby would have been home from the bar long before a killer could track her down and run her off the road. Did Diane file a police report?"

"Let me check." I searched the database for Diane's address, and sure enough, Diane had made a report. "Dang, how did we miss that?"

"We didn't miss it, we found it late. Point: Diane poisoned Ruby with bleach. Maybe."

"Counter-point: I bet once Forensics is through with the bleach bottle, we won't have Diane's fingerprints on it."

"So you think..."

"I think Ruby did it herself to throw us off or to delay release from the hospital."

"Point: Diane inserted herself into the investigation."

"Counter-point: honestly, I could see her defense attorney saying she wanted the thrill of being part of the investigation. It goes with her lying about the work. She's a crime scene fiend, and proof shows she lies about being at and working crime scenes. And from what Ruby's mother says, they live in a fantasy world."

"Crap. Point: Diane's blue shirt."

"Counter-point: also easy to plant. Let me call IT about the phone."

I called the phone tech, Kyle, who was working on Ruby's phone. He said there were no email exchanges between her and Clive, no text messages, no photos, nothing to suggest she was in a relationship with him. He said there were only a few photos on the app, but when he looked, there was a cloud storage service with photos of the two women. Going through that would take a second warrant, and he'd already asked.

"So where are we headed with this? Did Ruby kill Benning and set-up Diane who previously killed Eunice?"

"Let's find out."

We questioned Diane. At first, we were friendly and let her calm down. But as soon as we started to press her on her lies, that was a different story.

"We checked with the morgue. You're a data entry clerk."

"No, a medicolegal death investigator. Whoever you spoke to must have been looking at the wrong name."

"We spoke to Patty-Lou Fisher. She says you two have been friends since you were girls."

"No, she's mistaken. She's old, senile. She gets confused is all."

"Did you kill anyone?"

"I never killed him, I never did, you have to believe me."

"What about someone else?"

"Wh–what do you mean?"

"I mean, who's in your freezer?"

Diane slumped in her chair and shook her head. She swallowed hard.

"Lawyer."

And that was the end of questioning. It didn't matter. We had her with a body in her freezer. Now we had to figure out Benning. And Ruby.

Scotty and I sat at our desks pouring over information and discussing theories. We finally came up with one that seemed to fit all the possibilities: Ruby killed Benning, then framed herself in such a way that it looked like Diane framed her. That's clever, in a twisted sort of way.

We occasionally dropped in to see Ruby. We collected her DNA, we talked to her about the crash, we even chatted about Clive. At no time did she ask how Diane was.

The evidence grew. We found Ruby's DNA on the coffee cup, along with Diane's. That Diane's was there meant at some point, Diane was drinking it and it wasn't poisoned. Then it was poisoned, and Ruby drank from it. It could be argued she poisoned it herself to frame Diane.

Nothing indicated Diane touched the Corning bottle, bit they did find Ruby's DNA.

Ruby's fingerprints were found on the plastic cup that had held Benning's blood.

We'd reviewed the footage from security cameras on buildings near The Grab Bar. No one followed either Ruby or Benning in or out.

We had the parking ticket for Ruby's car on a street not far from Benning's place. That put her car there at the right time. One of our innocuous questions was about loaning out her car. She assured us, she never let anyone else drive her car.

We aren't sure how Ruby knew where to stab Benning with such efficiency, but it might show up on an internet search of her laptop.

We knew Diane was envious, but so was Ruby. Ruby was outraged that Diane had left her. A very common motive. Ruby had opportunity: the parking ticket sealed that one. And means? She admitted seeing Benning that night, and to previously being at his house. Piece by piece, it fit together.

When a dog walker found a bloody size six shoe–in fact, the dog found it and brought it to the dog walker–we were able to test the DNA. It matched.

Epilog

It took the coroner three days to thaw the body in the freezer. It was Eunice, and she had a puncture to her neck. When we advised Diane's lawyer, Diane reached out to us.

"We are sitting here today with Diane Emerat and her lawyer…"

"Lidia Carlisle."

"I'm Detective Francine Temple."

"I am Detective Scott O'Reilly. We understand you have something to say to us?"

Diane looked at her lawyer, who nodded.

"Ruby killed Eunice. Stabbed her. This was two, maybe 2 and half years ago. She …ssshk. Right in the neck. Eunice didn't care for Ruby, I guess she told her that one too many times. I admit I moved her to the freezer. Had to give away all the food that was in there, to make room. Eunice was pretty small, so it was easy enough."

"Why'd you cover her in ice?"

"Well, one, to stop the smell. But did you know, cryonics allows a person to be revived after appearing to die? You see, we don't actually die when the doctors say we die. We die when our soul leaves the body, which takes upwards of three days. So, if you freeze the body within three days, you trap the soul and keep the person alive. When they are thawed out, voila! They are alive and you can fix them or do whatever."

"Do whatever?"

"Yeah, like fix the wound, or cure the cancer. Whatever."

"We've thawed Eunice out. She's dead."

"Detectives, my client's religious beliefs should not be a source of entertainment for you."

"Were you cashing her social security checks?"

"Yes, but I was saving the money for when she came back to us."

"Okay, let's park that. Let's talk about Clive Benning."

"May I first confer with my client?"

"No, that's alright Lidia, I'll talk. I had nothing to do with Clive. I'd never even heard of him, never met him, didn't kill him. I know you're still digging stuff up. Have you checked Ruby's smart watch? It had GPS on it. I used it to watch where she was going."

"We haven't found a smartwatch."

"Doesn't matter. It's all saved to the cloud. Good old cloud. There's an app, I'll give my lawyer the password. It shows everywhere Ruby has been since I gave her the watch two years ago. She could never quite figure out how I knew where she was all the time."

After a few more denials of killing Clive, the lawyer shut us down. That was the end of interviewing Diane.

It took 20 minutes for Lidia to give us the user name and password for the smartwatch tracker app. And wow,

Diane was right. It is a very detailed list of everywhere the user went, for 27 months.

It started on Ruby's birthday, and spent most of the time at Ruby's house and Peachtree Fabrications. Ruby would be hard pressed to say this wasn't her.

On the Wednesday morning before Benning died, it showed Ruby going to Peachtree for 8:00 a.m., staying until 5:00 p.m., and then going to Mildred's.

There was a one hour and forty-three minute stop at the Vlasker Motel, which she had not told us about, and then at 9:03 p.m., she went to The Grab Bar. At 12:30 a.m., she parked near Benning's house. Over an hour later, she drove away. Ruby's watch stopped on Old Weller Road at 2:17 a.m.

We presented the evidence to the prosecutor, who agreed that a charge of first degree murder was in order. We'd figure out Eunice's death in due course.

"What do you think, Francine? Will she be happy? Sad? Deluded?"

I laughed. "Surprised. I think she'll be surprised."

Scotty and I headed to the Little Bluff Hospital with a couple of uniformed officers. I have to say, when we saw Ruby sitting at the entrance, we were both surprised.

"Going somewhere?" Scotty made that sound so sarcastic, I almost burst out laughing.

"Dr. Galliano said I'm okay to go home. Waiting for my taxi."

"We can give you a ride, if you'd like." I smiled at Ruby and her eyes lit up.

"Yes, please."

I signaled to uniform who came over, stood her up, and handcuffed her.

"What is this? No way! No effing way! You can't arrest me."

Effing? Such language. "You are under arrest, Ruby. Take her to Homicide."

She moaned and protested and wiggled and squirmed, but was eventually loaded into the cruiser and driven away.

"You know, she almost had us."

"Almost doesn't count. We've got her cold."

"Yes. Way to go, partner." Scotty high-fived me. "I'd suggest we go out for a drink to celebrate but... How's Sam doing?"

"She's doing alright. They saw some spots on her lungs which might be a result of the chemo treatments. So they are suspended until the lung thing gets straightened out."

"She'll be okay."

I nodded. "Are you kidding? Sam is still doing really well. We've got Diane Emerat and Ruby Fisher both locked up now. Everything is fantastic."

"Fan-tash-tic!"

That was Scotty's worst Cher ever, and it made me laugh.